CRASS

GRASS

C.Z. NIGHTINGALE

 PENGUIN BOOKS

PENGUIN BOOKS

Published by the Penguin Group
Penguin Books Ltd, 80 Strand, London WC2R 0RL, England
Penguin Putnam Inc., 375 Hudson Street, New York, New York 10014, USA
Penguin Books Australia Ltd, 250 Camberwell Road, Camberwell, Victoria 3124, Australia
Penguin Books Canada Ltd, 10 Alcorn Avenue, Toronto, Ontario, Canada M4V 3B2
Penguin Books India (P) Ltd, 11 Community Centre, Panchsheel Park, New Delhi – 110 017, India
Penguin Books (NZ) Ltd, Cnr Rosedale and Airborne Roads, Albany, Auckland, New Zealand
Penguin Books (South Africa) (Pty) Ltd, 24 Sturdee Avenue, Rosebank 2196, South Africa

Penguin Books Ltd, Registered Offices: 80 Strand, London WC2R 0RL, England

www.penguin.com

First published 2003
1

Set in 10.5/15 pt Sabon
Typeset by Rowland Phototypesetting Ltd, Bury St Edmunds, Suffolk
Made and printed in England by Clays Ltd, St Ives plc

British Library Cataloguing in Publication Data
A CIP catalogue record for this book is available from the British Library

ISBN 0–141–31634–9

To Emily and Morag

With thanks to Carl Dowling,
Isabel Crozier, Aysha Choudhury,
Kian Momtahan, Linda Obeng-Frimpomah
and Fatima and Haleema Rouf.

CONTENTS

1

THEN
WAY BACK
LONG AGO

That white transit was trouble. I had a bad feeling about it the moment I saw it parked under the ratty trees, where the road bends away from the canal. Between me and the footbridge. Right in my way.

I crouched down for a second behind one of the heaps of rubble that used to be the old mattress factory. Guys, loads of them, crowded round the transit. I couldn't see what they were up to, but I knew it was bad, really bad.

I did not want to walk past the transit. I did not want to see what those guys were up to. And I did not want them to see me. But if I was going to cut over the footbridge into Martineau Street, I was going to have to walk right past them. And if I turned back now, I was dead.

I was late for work. Again. And Warwick was on my case. He's the boss's son and he's only a year older than me, but he carries on like he owns the shop. I'd been chatting away to my mates Natalie and Kendra in the art room and totally lost track of time. No way was I going to make it to the shop by half past four if I went back to the main road now. And if I didn't make it, Warwick was going to kill me.

Get outa here! said a voice inside my head. *Run!* But I hadn't come this far to turn back now. I was halfway along Canal Road. Halfway to the footbridge. Why would those guys round the van bother about me? Round here you learn to look the other way while you are still in your buggy. You can say, 'I never saw nothin',' before your third birthday. I only had to keep my head down and look the other way and they'd never even notice I was there.

Studying the ground round my left foot, I scurried towards the bridge. It was quiet. Too quiet. I could hear my trainers scuffing on the loose stones. As I got near the van, the skin between my shoulder blades began to prickle. The muscles in my calves twitched – but I knew not to run. Stay cool, Caryn, I told myself. In two minutes you'll be on the bridge and outa here.

So why did I look back? I still can't answer that one. Two, three more steps, and I would have been over the canal and safe in the streets the other side. I would have saved myself untold heartache and grief. But what did I do? Right up on the crown of the bridge, where I stood out like a pointing finger against the sky, I had to turn round and look at the white transit.

Someone was getting a kicking. A real going over. Two guys were slamming into a dark shape that lay huddled-up on the ground. They were really going for it, giving it everything they'd got. Arms flying through the air. Bodies jerking backwards with each kick. Then one guy leaps into the air and crashes down on top of it with both feet.

The shape on the ground lies still. Its arms are wrapped over its head. Its knees are drawn up to its chin.

It's only a kid. About sixteen. The same age as me. They've tipped his stuff out of his schoolbag – they'd have done that first, to scare him, to have some fun. His folders lie on the ground, two red, one yellow. White squares of paper are strewn across the grass.

Nine or ten guys urge them on with arms and fists. Balaclavas and baseball caps hide their faces. In their shiny black combat jackets they all look the same. As they move, their jackets swing open showing flashes of Day-Glo orange lining. They look like exotic beetles. Poisonous ones.

Then they back off a bit and wait.

The shape begins to move. It gathers its limbs together. It begins to push itself upwards. First hips, then shoulders, and last its head.

'NO! NO!' I shout silently across the space between us. 'STAY STILL! STAY DOWN!' But it doesn't hear. The beetles stand back when it starts to move. They watch it struggle. They let it hope. Then, when it has dragged itself up on to all fours, another wild burst of kicking knocks it back down again.

One guy isn't joining in the fun. He is lounging against the front of the van. He has a fag in his hand, but he isn't smoking it. If he is interested in what is going on, it doesn't show. He never moves a muscle. But when the kid on the ground falls back down he pushes himself off the van and walks over to the action. In his hand is a baseball bat.

The beetles close in tight round him. I see the bat whirl through the air, but I don't see it land. When the group separates again there is a dark stain on the ground. The kid's papers are no longer white. They are red.

Then suddenly he spins round, quick as a startled cat, and looks straight at me – just as if I had called his name. Which I had, in a way. Because I have a power. I only have to look at the back of someone's head and they turn round. In the street, in cars, even on passing buses, strangers turn round when I give them my look. And I had made him turn, by looking, when I should have been outa there long ago.

But that was it. Just a quick Polaroid of a man with a ponytail, in T-shirt and jeans. Then I took off from the bridge. I spread my arms like wings. My jacket flapped behind me. I swear, for a second, I flew!

No need to hurry now. I could take my time. I had a cast-iron excuse for Warwick. Just let him start! Just let him open his big mouth once! I checked out the shops in Martineau Street, but I couldn't get interested in the mags in Irmak's. I didn't even want to know about the new nail-art shop. In the end, I bought a can of 7-UP and propped myself up on a concrete planter for a ciggie. My hand was shaking so much it took me about half an hour to light it!

Then brakes scream – right in my ear. A red Nissan swivels to a halt right in front of me. The Toyota Jeep behind it swerves out of the way and only just misses the black Merc coming in the opposite direction. The cars behind stand on their brakes. Everyone is screaming and yelling and hooting. I'm on my feet to check the action and that's when I see it. A white transit, rolling towards me, straight into the traffic, on the wrong side of the road.

When it is opposite me it stops dead. The man with the ponytail leans out of the window and eyeballs me. I stare right back into eyes as hard as screw heads.

He's hard core all right! Ears bristling with rings and studs. About twenty chains round his neck. A ratty ripped T-shirt shows off his tattoos – a spider web all over one arm, and a collar of roses and thorns two inches thick on the chicken skin of his neck.

He doesn't say a word. Just looks. Takes my details. Files me for future reference. He is a total nutter. I will know him anywhere – and he will know me.

When he's seen enough, he bumps two wheels of the transit up on to the kerb and scoots along into the traffic until he skids round the corner into Garden Row. A piece of cloth is caught in the rear doors and hangs down over the number plate. Some joker has scrawled 'Stevie Wonder washed this van', in huge letters in the dust.

Warwick was doing three things at once, as usual – minding the till, pricing pet food and shouting into his mobile.

'Nah! Nah, man! With them wide wheels, right! Right. Gotcha! OK! Gotta go now! Call me in ten, yeah!'

He jabbed a finger at his watch when I fell through the door – and kept jabbing until he had finished his phone call.

Then he started, at full volume. 'What kept you? And it better be good. You're takin' liberties, right. You hear what I'm saying? I had to cover for you. I got deliveries to make, not hang round waiting for you to decide to turn up!'

I let him go on – to ease the pressure on his brain. Then I told him. About the battering. And how gutted I was.

He wasn't impressed. All he said was, 'What was he, Black or Asian?'

'I couldn't see. I was too far away.'

Warwick gave me a slitty-eyed look. Then he said, 'I don't know why you're gettin' so worked up. It ain't like it's ever gonna happen to you.'

June's bulk lurched along the aisle towards us. I held my breath. Warwick could moan. June could sack me. June was the boss.

'Get outa here, will ya,' said June, turning to Warwick. 'Get them deliveries done. The girl doesn't need you belly-aching.' He took my hand in his, opened it flat, placed two Flakes on to my palm, folded my fingers over them and held them there for a second. 'Make yourself a cup of tea. June will mind the till.'

I didn't need telling twice.

The tea was sweet and soothing. I fed a Flake into my face. Get a grip, Caryn, I told myself. Time to forget it now. Put it behind you. I unwrapped the other Flake and settled down on a pile of evening papers to think about Craig.

Hunger wipes your brain. I was so starving by the time I finished work I could have taken a bite out of the counter. The shop's always mad on Friday and I was rushed off my feet. All I wanted was my sofa, an Americano with extra pepperoni and chips, my dog and *Friends*. Outside, it was getting dark and it looked like rain. I zipped my jacket right up to my chin and set off towards the main road.

The footsteps came from nowhere. One minute – nothing. The next – there they were. Heavy, plonking footsteps, right on my heels. I walked faster – and they walked faster too. I slowed down – so did they. Panic looped through my guts. I could almost feel Rosie's breath on my neck – it had to be him – the man with the rosy tattoo. Coming after me again. Who else would it be?

I didn't turn round. I didn't want to look into Rosie's steely eyes. Whatever was going to happen, no way was I going to turn round and meet it!

A throaty voice growled in my ear, 'Caryn!'

A shudder, like an electric shock, went right through me and I jumped! I swear, my feet came right off the ground. But at the same time I knew that voice. I whirled round. There was Craig, his face split open by an enormous grin.

'Craig! You moron!' I shouted. 'Creeping up on me like that. I nearly died of fright.'

Craig works in Laser, the dry-cleaner up the road, and he comes into the shop on his way to the rec for vitamin drinks and bananas. He's down the rec most nights, in the gym or in the pool. Sometimes he's passing the shop as I'm leaving and we walk down the road together. Once I asked him to play frisbee with Mango, and he's turned up at the park a couple of times since then. He's crazy about my dog and she worships him.

I started swimming again because of him. If I see him in the pool I'll say my arm's dropping in my backstroke or something stupid like that, and we might have chat and a coffee – but he's never phoned me. Never even said, 'See y'around.' Natalie and Kendra swear he's my boyfriend, and I wish he was, but we're just mates.

'Hey! Caryn! Relax, will you?' said Craig. 'I didn't have

you down as the nervous type.' He stretched an arm round my shoulders and gave me a quick squeeze. The way he jerked his arm back again you'd think I was covered in prickles.

He smelled of chlorine and fabric conditioner. I love his smell. I breathed it in as hard as I could. I wanted him to put his arm round me again. Right round me. I wanted him to pull me close to him and hold me tight. It was the first time he had ever touched me, and I didn't want it to stop there.

We were already at the green. The streets were dark and autumny, and slippery with wet leaves. We would soon be at the main road, and if I didn't do something quickly, Craig would jog off to the gym and I wouldn't see him again for days, maybe even weeks. And by that time he would have forgotten that he'd touched me. If I was ever going to get anywhere with him, I had to move things on now.

Why had he put his arm round me when he did? Because I panicked. Because I had jumped out of my skin. Well, I could be panicked again, couldn't I? I could tell him what happened down by the canal. I could make it well scary, couldn't I?

So I told him about the white van. And about the guys in black jackets. And what I saw them doing to the shape on the ground.

'They were like wild animals,' I said. 'They just tore into him. There was blood everywhere. They must have broken every bone in his body. This one guy ran at his head and kicked it just like it was a football. And then, when they'd finished, they came after me. I swear I had to run for my life.' I must have made it sound good because I shuddered as I said it.

It didn't work. Craig was interested all right, but not in the way I wanted – not in me. He kept going on and on about the guys in the van. How many were there? Did I get a good look at them? Did they have billiard cues? Baseball bats? Belts? Would I know them if I saw them again? He was being really off with me now, hanging back behind me, like he wasn't really with me at all. I even had to turn round to answer his questions.

We were just about at the main road. I wasn't going to give up now. I told him about Rosie following me down the street. And about all the cars in the road nearly crashing and him not turning a hair. And about him eyeballing me from the window of the transit, and slashing his finger across his throat before driving off. So the last one was a lie? It sounded good.

I'd properly scared myself by the time I'd finished, but if Craig noticed, he didn't show it. All he said was, 'How do you know it was him? There must be a hundred white transits in Bow.'

And how many of them would be chasing me down the street? Doh! I'm like, 'It was him, Craig. I'd know him anywhere.'

'I bet you were on the phone to all your mates right away?' Craig was still dawdling along behind me. He was looking everywhere but at me.

'No,' I said. 'I only told you. And Warwick in the shop. I told him because I was late for work.'

'What about your mum? You gonna tell your mum?'

'Mum!' I shouted. 'You gotta be joking. Mum'd have me down the police station in two seconds flat – and then what? If I grass, nobody I know will ever speak to me ever again. So. End of story. Right.'

Craig grinned at me. 'Right.' Then he goes, 'Come out with me Saturday. There's a good band at The Waterman. Christian at the rec's brother's DJ-ing.'

I'm like, 'Er – m . . . Yeah . . . Maybe . . . OK . . . All right then,' as if I had to think about it.

'I'll see you outside The Waterman at nine o'clock.' He gave my shoulder another squeeze and he was off.

I ran all the way home. I couldn't wait to phone Layla. And Natalie and Kendra. I couldn't believe how weird life was – how it had taken those scum around the white van to make Craig realize that he did care about me after all.

2
BIG LIP

When I first started at June's I needed a dictionary. And a map. I could lay my hands on the P G Tips and the cornflakes from day one, no problem, but amchoor? Asafoetida? Awame? – I didn't have a clue. The first few days were mental, but after a bit it all fell into place. Whatever you need, I can go straight to it now.

Junior Binn's Exotic Produce and Health Foods – that's what it says on the sign in red, green and gold letters. What it means is weird stuff from all over the world. You name it, June's got it, crammed on to the shelves, rattling on strings across the aisles and piled on trestles in the street – and weird types come from all over to buy it. I never touch any of it – except the Venezuelan sucking mangoes. They're so brilliant I named my dog after them.

I work here Tuesday evening, Friday evening and all day Saturday. I never thought I would, but I like it. I like chatting to the customers. I like June's mad new lines. And I like the vegetably, earthy, spicy smell. I could walk round the shop blindfold and I would know exactly where I was by the smell. Sometimes I just breathe it in. Sometimes it's so strong I want to skin it up and smoke it.

The downside is Warwick moaning on all the time.

'Hey, guess what, right?' I shouted. I was in the back, unpacking bottles of pasta sauce. Warwick'd been on the till all morning and he was in a bad mood. I was trying to get him to lighten up. 'There's a tribe in the Amazon rainforest who eat tarantulas. They barbecue them. Live. I thought . . .'

'Yeah, yeah. Very funny.' Warwick didn't let me finish. 'You taking your break? There's things I gotta do.'

He hates being stuck in the shop. The idea is he gets out on Saturdays when I'm here, but June is at the cash and carry and Olly, who does a couple of hours heavy lifting, hasn't showed up yet.

'My break's at eleven. I'm not taking it a minute before.' I walk down to the till. I don't want to shout myself hoarse.

'Take it early,' goes Warwick. 'I wanna be out that door the minute Dad gets back.'

'Yeah?' I say. 'And what about when June finds out there was only one of us in the shop? He'll go ballistic. What then?'

Warwick chews his lip – which he does when he's thinking how to get what he wants. His lip has grooves in it, where his front teeth slot in. Then he remembers it's me he wants to do something for him and he rolls a big smile on to his face. 'I'll tell Dad it was me. You won't get into trouble. Go on, Caz. It's urgent!'

Yeah. Right. It's always urgent. And what about my morning? That doesn't matter, I suppose. It's going to drag on forever if I take an early break.

'Leave it out, Warwick,' I snap. 'My break's at eleven. All right?'

'All right! Forget it! Twenty minutes! That's all I'm arksin you – twenty little minutes. I'd do the same for you. You know that, don't you? You wait till you want something. You'll . . .'

He's winding himself up and he'll go on and on till he gets what he wants. Usually I give in. Why give myself grief? He is the boss's son after all.

But then, before I can say anything, June is sliding through the door, trays of canned beans towered up to his chin. 'More of these in the van, son,' he says. 'Caryn, mind the till while we unload.'

'Then Caryn's taking her break,' goes Warwick, quick as a flash, 'so I can get out. Innit, Caryn?'

A cup of coffee was waiting for me in the store, on top of a stack of canned chickpeas. An unwrapped Kit-Kat lay on a plate, with a knife and a fork on either side of it. Very hilarious. Ha ha. The coffee was grey and scummy with blobby islands of half-melted granules and powdered milk floating on top. I took a mouthful – and spat it straight back into the cup. This coffee had never seen the inside of a kettle. It wasn't even lukewarm. Fishbrain had made it straight from the hot tap – without even bothering to let it run hot.

Right, that was it! I'd had enough! My break started from the moment I had a proper cup of steaming hot coffee in my hand. I filled the kettle right up to the top, shifted the boxes round to make myself a place to sit and settled down to wait for it to boil.

Someone had left a *Gazette* on the worktop – I started to flick through it for pictures of people I know. Warwick fussed in and out, getting his precious camera and all its stuff together. He loves that camera. It's only an old rubbish one from Brick Lane, but he picks it up like it was a kitten or something. He'll even give it a stroke sometimes, with the tips of his fingers, before settling it down in his going-out bag.

Then I saw it! It didn't register at first. I was checking the wedding pictures and something went click in my brain. I didn't even know what I was looking for as I flicked back through the pages, then there it was, hidden away between a story about a Chinese Elvis impersonator, and mating hamsters who kept the neighbours awake at night.

LOCAL YOUTH ATTACKED

A young Asian student was attacked and viciously assaulted on his way home from school last Friday.

The victim was lying unconscious in a pool of blood on a lonely street when he was discovered by a passing jogger who alerted the emergency services.

Kobir Chowdhury (16) who lives at 72, Annie Besant House, Antilles Street, was rushed to the London Hospital where he is being treated for head injuries. His condition is described as 'serious'.

Police want to speak to anyone who witnessed the attack, which took place on Canal Road, at approximately 4.30 p.m. on Friday. They suspect that the attack, which a spokesman described as 'exceptionally vicious', may have had a racist motive.

Canal Road appears in the air in front of my eyes – ghostly, see through, like an etching on a wineglass. the huddled figure on the ground, still as a stone. The guys in their combat jackets piling into the transit. Police cars. Ambulances. Then the road is empty. The dark figure is gone.

I stare at the newspaper. What's going on? This isn't right! Where is the white transit? The gang in the black jackets? Where is Rosie? Why is there nothing about them? The police should have picked them up by now. Shouldn't they? Shouldn't they?

I try to read the report again. I can't make any sense of it. I read slowly, checking each word off with my finger. But it still won't say what I want it to say!

Police want to speak to anyone who witnessed the attack. Yes! Enough people must have seen what was going on. There's always someone jogging or walking the dog by the canal. And there are houses just the other side. Someone must have seen something.

The words are like jumping beans on the page. I read the report one more time, trying to get the letters to rearrange themselves into the words I want to see – arrested, held for questioning, helping the police with their enquiries. But it's no use. Nobody saw the white transit. Nobody saw the gang who kicked the shit out of the boy on the ground. Nobody saw the man with the ponytail and the tattoos. Only me.

His name is Kobir. Kobir Chowdhury. He lives in Antilles Street, just round the corner from the shop. If those scum hadn't done what they did to him, I would probably have met him on the bridge.

'Car-yn!' It was Warwick. 'Get outa there! You've had at least twenty minutes! What d'you think you're playing at?'

He changed his tune when he saw my face. 'Wassup, Caz? You look terrible.'

I pushed the paper over to him.

'This what you saw, you reckon?' He gave the paper a flick, like he was getting rid of a crumb. 'Nah, man! "Condition serious." They always say that. He'll be all right. The guy's gonna be all right.'

'Caryn! Caryn! Over here!' Layla was shouting across the packed caff. One arm waved madly, the other was hooked over the back of the chair next to her. Only Layla would even think of hanging on to an empty seat in Callegari's at lunchtime.

The caff was bursting at the seams. Market traders were piling in off the street and crowding round the door until someone budged up enough to let them sit down. Layla's bright red T-shirt stood out a mile against all the sludgy anoraks and old woolly jumpers. It was her favourite, with the leaping dragon on the front. The dragon's scales looked like gold and black fingernails.

Layla's my best mate. Of course Natalie and Kendra are mates too, but not like Layla. I've probably spent more time at Layla's house than my own – ever since Bridget, her mum, got fed up with waiting outside the infants for my mum to show up and decided that, in future, I was coming home with her. I stayed there so often that I even had my own bed in Layla's room.

I fought my way through the crush. Everyone who comes to Callegari's knows everyone else and they were all shouting their news across the room. Sonia Callegari was standing in the middle, taking orders above the din. 'All right, my love. What'll it be? We've got some nice liver today – just how you like it. With onions. And calabrese. That's broccoli to you, my love. And the chicken for you, my dear? Fried or grilled?' Layla and I've been coming here ever since we discovered Mrs Callegari's bread pudding in year eight. Layla doesn't have it any more, but I do. I shouted my order across to Sonia.

Layla grabbed my hand and pulled me down beside her. 'Hey! So what about this Craig then? Is he nice-looking? Who does he look like? You like dark, innit? Is he dark? What car's he got? Where d'you find him? Why didn't you tell me about him before?'

I'm like, 'Layla! I did tell you! He's the gorgeous one I met at the rec. Lay, he's really . . .' but then I stop dead. I don't know how to tell Layla about Craig. Layla goes for looks. And labels. And wheels. Her boyfriends wear designer for going out, and borrow their brother's cars.

Craig's not like that. He's not even that good-looking. Not in the way Layla means. He's as thin as a stick. His jeans skim from hipbone to hipbone without touching his tummy. His face is all knobs and bumps. But he's got a big, squishy, sexy mouth I can't wait to kiss. And he does have muscles. Big muscles in his arms, like lemons.

Why couldn't I just say, I think he's sexy and we have a laugh and he likes playing frisbee with my dog? It sounded fine in my head, but I knew Layla wouldn't be impressed. So what I said was, 'He's got fair hair and these weird, sexy eyes and he dresses sporty. And he works in a shop, but he's going to college next year.' Which was nearly all lies, except the bit about Craig's eyes. They are light, light grey, silver almost, with a dark ring round the outside, and when he is worked up about something, the dark ring gets darker.

Sonia plonked a slab of bread pudding on the table in front of me. It was brown and rough and lumpy. It looked like our hall carpet just inside the front door. As soon as I set eyes on it, my throat tightened and I knew there was no way I was going to get it down. Thinking about it made me gag and I shoved it away to the other side of the table.

Layla's fingertips rested on my wrist. 'Caryn. What's up? You're acting weird. You're not talking to me. Warwick giving you a hard time?'

I've never, ever been able to get anything past Layla. She always knows exactly what I'm feeling, sometimes before I know I'm feeling it myself. I might as well have an LCD on my forehead!

'No,' I say. 'No worse than normal.'

'So are we going shopping, or what?'

Shopping! I'd asked Layla to come lunchtime shopping with me to find something to wear for my date in the evening. I'd only been up half the night thinking about it – how to look cool and sexy, but not like I'd tried too hard. But now! Now I had seen that bit in the *Gazette* – how was I going to get my head round tops and trousers and skirts? It was bursting with pictures of Canal Road. The dark shape on the ground. The gang in their shiny combat jackets. It was like I had a video playing inside my skull, permanently stuck on pause.

'Yeah!' I said. 'Course we are!'

'So what sort of stuff is Mr Craig weird-eyes into then? Short and sexy? Skintight? Long and floaty? I thought we'd go to Roxanne's. Her stuff's OK. Personally, I prefer Idiom myself, but Roxanne's more your style.'

The plastic table top had a pattern of brown squares with orange spirals inside. I was tracing round the spirals with my finger. Once I had started, I had to do every spiral in a square. Like jumping cracks between the paving slabs when I was a little kid. If I didn't do every single one, the bears would come out and get me!

'Look at this pattern,' I said. 'It looks dead modern, doesn't it? But I bet it's original seventies.' I missed a beat, then I said, 'I saw someone being beaten up yesterday.'

'So?' said Layla. 'It's the national pastime round here.'

'He's hurt bad,' I said. My finger was still following the orange spiral round and round. 'It was even in the *Gazette* today. It said his condition was serious.'

'So?' said Layla. 'They're all animals. Let them get on with it, I say.' She was redoing her lipstick. She can slick it on and roll it round her lips without looking, and it doesn't smudge and it matches her T-shirt exactly. When she had finished she jumped to her feet. 'That better not be what's bothering you, Caryn, what the local low lifes are up to. Let them get on with it. It's not your problem. We've got shopping to do . . .'

3

SHOWING NO LOVE

Craig was leaning against the wall outside The Waterman. The minute I saw him I felt clumsy and frumpy – all bits and pieces that didn't fit together. My legs looked like broomsticks in my new skirt. My top was showing miles more midriff than it did in the shop and my arms flapped by my sides like they had grown an extra six inches. Then I was close enough to see his face . . . and none of it mattered any more!

He took my hand and said, 'I thought I'd wait for you out here. I didn't want you walking in there alone.'

He'd gelled his hair up into spikes and there was a drop of blood on his chin. He'd put on a new shirt too – it still had the fold-lines in it from the packet. I wanted to reach out and smooth it down flat across his chest, but I didn't dare. Just looking at him a tingle started at the back of my knees and ziggled all the way up to my neck.

The Waterman was buzzing. The DJ was just starting and everyone was running round getting drinks in and checking out who was there. Kendra must have been watching the door because we had only just got through it when I saw her watermelon head pumping through the crowd towards us. Not that you could miss it. Kendra's head is big and round and totally bald – except for a slick of hair on top which she dyes gold and gells into swirls. She came to a stop right in front of Craig and gave him the once over. She's got no shame. She'd have turned him round and upside down if she could.

Craig was so cool. He just said, 'Hi, Kendra,' and let her carry on looking.

'We've got those tables over there. All of us. We can just about squeeze you in,' she said pointing to where our lot had taken over a corner of the room.

'Not tonight, Kendra,' said Craig, pulling me towards him. 'This is our first date. I'm keeping Caryn to myself tonight.'

Kendra saw the look on my face and rolled her eyes round in her head. 'Where have I heard that before? Just watch it then, or you'll end up an old married couple like those two!' She nodded in the direction of Natalie and her boyfriend, Reuben, who were scrunched up over a table the other side of the bar. Natalie's long, blonde hair hung down in front of them like a curtain – her personal Keep Off sign. Kendra gave a 'whatever next' shrug. 'I'll leave you to it then. Have fun! See ya later!'

'When are you getting your hair done like that?' said Craig as soon as the crowd had swallowed her up. Then he reached out and touched my flick-ups and said, 'Only joking! Your hair looks nice. You done something to it?'

Tonight I was here to dance. I wanted to be right in there with the music. I wanted everyone to see Craig and me together. But Craig had other ideas. He meant it when he said he was keeping me to himself. He got our drinks, then he took my hand and shoved his way through the crowd. He kept going until he'd found us a table right at the back, squashed up against the fire exit, where it was nearly dark and smelled of toilet cleaner. I had to wrestle my chair out from under the table before I could get my bum down on it.

'Craig!' I said. 'What's going on? There were loads of tables near the front.'

He made a grab for my hand. 'I thought you'd want to be alone?' he said. 'You know. Get to know each other a bit.'

Fine! If that was what he wanted. We'd do it his way. I didn't have a problem with that. There were a thousand questions I was dying to ask him. After all, what did I know about him? That he keeps himself fit. He's fed up with Laser. He supports West Ham. We'd chatted a lot, but we'd never really talked.

So why wouldn't he talk to me then? He didn't want to know. He mumbled answers to my questions: yes, a sister. Older. Married. With kids. Girl and boy. Mum? What about her? Dad? What dad? . . . But me? He never asked me one single thing. He didn't even try to get to know me. He wasn't even looking at me. His eyes flick-flicked all round the room, anywhere but at me. And all the time he was throwing punches with one hand and catching them with the other. Slap. Slap. It got on my nerves. In the end I felt like one of those saddos who turn up on your doorstep asking questions about spray polish and diet drinks. I shut up.

The evening was turning out to be a total disaster. It was doing my head in, and it was all Craig's fault. Why had he asked me out in the first place if he didn't want to talk to me and he didn't want to dance?

Christian's brother was bang on it. He knew how to

work the crowd, get them going. Everyone was on their feet, dancing, swaying and jigging about. I dragged Craig up too. I needn't've bothered. He's not the worst dancer I've ever seen – he stays with the music, but he throws his arms and legs around as if he wants to get rid of them and he doesn't move his body at all. That wouldn't have worried me, but his face said that he was hating it, and his eyes were still flick-flicking round the room. And I hate that! I hate it when I'm dancing with a boy and he's checking out all the other girls in the room at the same time.

I was fed up with him now. I didn't care. I told him to get me another drink and went to find Kendra. I never feel bad for long when I am with Kendra. She was dancing with Paulo, one of her mates from art. They were looking good together, but I told him to get lost – not in a bad way – so I could dance with her.

Kendra was born to dance. She dances as easily as she breathes, and when I dance with her I can really let go. I feel the music under my feet like the floor is one huge speaker – lifting me, carrying me, turning me, and I go with it – as far as it wants me to go. And did I go for it? I danced my tits off! I wanted Craig to know what he could have if he wanted . . . Yes! But I wanted to show him that I could have a good time without him too.

'Where's lover boy then?' Kendra didn't wait for an answer. She grabbed hold of me and stuck her face up close to my ear. 'That geezer over there by the bar's been staring at your Craig. He was watching you when you were dancing. Turn round. He's the one in the leather jacket, in the corner. He hasn't taken his eyes off Craig once.'

I turned round. Slowly. Craig was still at the bar, fiddling around with his change. The man in the leather jacket was over the other side. Dark hair, plastered down flat. Meaty red face. Stubble. Nothing special. He was watching Craig – not staring, but watching. I could look straight at him from where I was, but there was a bunch of people between him and Craig. Meatface took another look at Craig, then stepped back behind them. He definitely didn't want to be seen.

Craig walked towards me carrying our drinks. Meatface made his move, came out of the crowd and towards Craig. Craig was looking at the drinks, trying not to spill them. Then he looked up and there was Meatface right in front of him. He stopped – dead! Meatface stopped too. The drinks slopped on to the floor. Nobody said a word. Craig just stood there, looking stupid. His hands were wet with Coke. Meatface sort of nodded at him, then carried on walking across the bar and out the door.

I rushed over to Craig. 'Who was that man? Why was he watching you? What did he want?'

Craig had put the drinks down on the nearest table. He was trying to dry his hands on the back of his jeans. He turned his back to me and the words squeezed out of him, 'What man?'

What man! What did he think he was playing at? 'The man in the leather jacket, of course, who's just gone out. Who almost bumped into you. I saw him!'

He muttered, 'I never saw no one,' still with his back to me.

I didn't believe I was hearing this. What was going on?

I wanted to hit him. 'Craig!' I shouted. 'Don't lie! I saw what happened! I saw that guy with my own eyes!'

He turned round and shouted back, right in my face, 'Leave it out, Caryn! I saw someone I didn't want to see, right. And he's gone now, so just leave it.' And he stomped off back to his corner by the fire doors.

We sat there at the back for ages. I was gutted. I could see a blur of bodies dancing and swaying against the light. Blurred because of the tears in my eyes. I kept my face turned away from Craig. After more ages, he touched my hand.

'She's something else when she dances, your friend, isn't she?' he said. 'Must be cos she's black, d'you think?'

Kendra! That was it! Our first date – he wouldn't talk to me, he wouldn't dance with me, he'd lied to me, we'd had a fight. And now he was talking about my friend! I didn't want to hear what he thought about Kendra's dancing. It was me he was supposed to have been watching, not Kendra. I was glad it was dark. I tipped my head back so my tears wouldn't spill over and stood up. It was time to pack it in and go home.

Craig stood up at exactly the same time. 'Look, Caryn,' he said, 'let's go. There's still people I don't want to see might be coming in here. It means I can't relax, so let's just get out, OK?'

Craig lightened up as soon as we left the pub. It was getting cold and I was shivering. He put his arm round me and pulled me close to him.

'I'm sorry, Caryn. It was that guy in the leather jacket. He was getting to me. He thinks I know something about him that I shouldn't, but I don't. You must hate me now?'

Go on then, I wanted to say. Who was he? What does he think you know? I was dying for him to tell me, but it would have to wait now. No way was I going to risk ruining this new mood.

'You're a good dancer, Caryn,' said Craig. 'When I said that about your mate, I meant you. You look nice when you dance. You look nice tonight. I've never seen you dressed up before. You're all sparkly.'

He was looking straight ahead when he spoke and, with a flash of white, his eyes slid slowly round to look at me. Then he pulled me over and looked right into my eyes and I looked right back into his and I felt like I did the first time I stood on the top board at the swimming pool, my toes curled over the end – and nothing in front of me and nothing underneath me but gut-clenching empty space . . . and I grabbed hold of him and I kissed him!

We just wandered. At first we stuck to the bright lights and traffic, but we soon found ourselves in quiet side streets, kissing and talking. I told him how Dad came all the way over from Germany to see me play my recorder in the school concert when Mum couldn't get time off work. And how, when he saw how often I was staying at Layla's, he never went back. I told him how gobsmacked everyone was when I won the chess tournament in year six because I was so crap at school. And how I nicked a box of cream eggs from Mumtaz' Minimart because Kendra bet me I wouldn't.

Craig opened right up. He told me about his mum – the original gypsy, he calls her, because she's always moving house. If it isn't one thing it is another. The house is too big. The flat is too small. The neighbours complain about the dog.

She doesn't like living next door to Pakis. And off they go.

'I'd just get to know my way to the sweet shop and we'd be moving on,' he said. That made me laugh, but it was sad, really. He ended up staying with his nan in Cubitt Town until they put the new rail link right through her house. His nan's his real mum, he says. He's living with his sister now, sharing a room with the baby.

Then we bought some chips and went back to mine. Craig was nervous, but I told him he didn't have to worry. Mum's never back till three on Saturday night. It's her night out with her mates.

Mango was hurling herself at the front door as I fumbled for my keys. She went mad with excitement when Craig called her, and when she saw him, she nearly weed herself. She's only a pup, rusty gold with a white throat and oversized pointy ears. Dad gave her to me a year ago to keep me company in the evening when Mum's at college and I love her to bits.

A note was clamped to the fridge door. Red arrows slashed into the page from each corner. 'Staying at Davina's. Food inside. Love Mum.'

Why does she bother with notes? I always know where she is, more or less. It's Davina's. Or college. Or Shiatsu. Or Flamenco. Or sometimes she's just out.

I ripped the note off the door and chucked it in the bin.

Craig grinned. 'Mum not coming back then?'

'She's staying over with her mate,' I said. 'But don't get any ideas. You're out of here in an hour.' But he was getting ideas. He liked me. And the tingle started at the back of my knees again.

I made us a coffee and looked for some music to get Craig to chill some more. He and Mango were wrestling for a rolled-up newspaper. Mango was snarling like she was in it for real. Her top lip was rolled back to the gum, showing her needly little front teeth. Her eyeballs were edged with white and she was flinging her head about like a mad thing. When Craig dropped the paper she jumped up on to the settee beside him and thrust her nose into his armpit and when I sat down next to him she growled at me. My own dog! It cracked us both up. I shoved her on to the floor and cuddled up to Craig, but she jumped back up again and tried her best to wriggle her way in between us. Craig couldn't move for laughing.

We listened to music, chatted, cuddled. The evening was turning out all right after all. I felt fuzzy with happiness. But then, when I told him it was time for him to go, Craig only had to go and spoil everything again. He pulled away from me and sat on the edge of the settee, cracking his knuckles and staring up at the china spaniel Mum uses to stop her paperbacks falling over. Then he said, 'You don't do bad things, do you, Caryn? Nickin' those cream eggs is the wickedest thing you ever done, right?'

Bad? Wicked! Where did that all come from? I didn't know where I was with Craig from one minute to the next. I didn't know what to say. I'd never even thought about it – bunking Environmental Studies? Putting Listerine on Dogbreath Doherty's desk? Doherty had real tears in her eyes when she saw the Listerine! – was that wicked?

'Ivor's watch,' I said, when I'd had time to think about it. 'Mum had this boyfriend called Ivor who was a right sleeze. I hated him. I nicked his Rolex off the bedside table and dropped it in the water tank in the loft.'

The tank was round and made of black plastic. The water inside was pitch black, but a skin of dust on top gave it a silvery gleam – like a big, blank eye. I only had to look at it and I felt funny inside. I held Ivor's watch just under the surface and let it hang there, a line of light pointing down into the blackness. Then I took my hand away. I never meant to let it go, I swear. But before I could grab it back it had gone! Disappeared! Like a hand had reached up from the depths and snatched it away from me. I was shaking all over when I climbed down the ladder out of the loft.

I did try to tell Craig. When I got to the bit about the hand, he nudged me in the ribs and smiled. Then he pointed a finger at me.

'Good one,' he said. 'I bet it wasn't a genuine Rolly.'

4
Touch LIFE

Mango and I were on the way to Dad's for Sunday lunch. I could have done with another hour in bed. I wanted to play last night – every single minute of last night – through in my head one more time, but Mango would have dug a hole underneath the door if I hadn't let her out. I always give Mango a long run on the way to Dad's, but this time I wanted to cut through Spindrift Street, find a seat in the park and tune back into last night. Mango wasn't having that. She wanted to carry on up the market to the Halal butchers because she once found a chicken leg there among all the rubbish in the gutter.

Craig wants to see me again! It was half past two when he left. We had been together five and a half hours and he still hadn't said anything and I was thinking, what happens now? Is that it? Then, when he was right out the door, he turns round and says, 'Do you want to come out again?' and I'm like, 'Yeah, if you want.' I'm seeing him Wednesday and I can't wait!

There was a blast of dinner and Babaa Maal as Dad opened the door. He's into world music now. West Africa this month. He says it will create the right mood in the cafe bar he and his business partner, aka Fat Uncle Al, are opening for the yuppies who are buying up all the old factories and warehouses behind the main road. He kissed me, handed me a glass of wine and turned back to his hob. He's doing the cooking at the cafe bar.

I put my arms round him and gave him a hug. He had a new lemony leathery smell and his sweater felt soft and expensive.

'Hey! How's my girl?' he said, reaching behind me to probe the bottom of a saucepan with a wooden spoon. 'I'm not usually honoured like this. Everything all right?'

'I'm fine,' I said. 'Hi, Jill. Romey still asleep?'

Jill looked up from her Mac. 'He should go another ten minutes if I'm lucky. I'll be with you then, Caryn, OK? Hi, anyway.'

I like Jill, but I have to say, she is a bit weird. Probably because she's a designer. She does things like wear green shoes with striped socks, and she's got loads of pairs of glasses with coloured frames – orange, lime green, purple. And she's taller than my dad.

Dad can talk about yuppies. He's a business man now. First it was Pete's Parts for Karts and now it's the cafe bar. He and Jill have a flat on the canal in a converted flour warehouse, which they call 'the loft'. It's one huge empty space, with rows of concrete pillars and a musty smell. And everything is right out there, except the toilet, which is in the stairwell. The washbasin and bath used to be out there too. You had everything you needed – towel rail, bath mat, a little table with soaps and bath oils and toothpaste – but no walls. I turned up early once and Jill was in the bath. She didn't care, just carried on splashing about as if she was alone. Anyway,

Jill's mum rebelled. She said she wasn't going to visit unless they put walls round the bathroom. So they did.

Dad says when they get it properly done up, I can live with them. I know that's what he wants, and it's what I want too, but not until I can have my own room. As it is, I stay over. I made them buy me a screen and I sleep behind that.

There was action behind the screen now. Romey was wide awake. He was giving his cot a pounding and shouting my name, 'Car! Car! Car!' He's been able to say it since he was ten months old. As soon as he saw me he squealed and stretched up his arms and I lifted him out of his cot for a cuddle. His face was still warm and crumpled from where he had been lying on it. I gave him a drink, changed him and lay down with him on the rug to give him a tickling.

'How's the cafe bar going?' I called to Dad, over Romey's shrieks and giggles and Babaa Maal.

'It's coming on fine. Right on target. That designer mate of Jill's I told you about is spot on. It's going to look like a dream inside when it's done. When did you last see it?'

'I haven't been there for a bit now. Have you come up with a name yet?'

'Not yet. Still working on it. Got a few ideas though. Hey, you sure my boy's still breathing. It sounds like he's choking to death!'

I was blowing raspberries on Romey's tummy and he was going mad and shouting, 'Mo! Mo!' in-between fits of giggles.

'He's good,' I said. 'He's having a great time.'

'He's a rascal, isn't he?' said Dad. Then he said, 'How's your new course?'

My course. He would have to get on to that. 'It's OK,' I said. 'Fine.'

I was doing AS levels, Media Studies and Psychology. I only chose them because they weren't the same boring old subjects I'd done for GCSE. I never wanted to stay on at school in the first place, but I didn't have a clue what else I wanted to do. And Mum and Dad got together to put the pressure on . . .

'Co-ome on. What's the problem?' said Dad.

The problem? It's bo-oring! You read something that's not about anything, you talk about it, then you write about it and then you read some more stuff. How pointless is that?

'No problem,' I said. 'It's OK. Really. What ideas?'

Dad was still working the same saucepan, feeling round the bottom of it with a wooden spoon. Then he lifted the spoon out of the pan, squinted at it and poked it with his finger. 'I'm thinking Romey's, after my boy. Here, Jill, taste this. Has it thickened yet? What d'you think?'

Jill was on it in a flash. 'We haven't come to any decision about names yet, Caryn. We've had one or two ideas, but nothing has been agreed.'

Excuse me! What does she think is going on here? Does she think I'm a kid or something? Jill does make life hard for herself. She's always falling over backwards to be fair to me. And I do know my dad. He's not exactly Mr Sensitive. Anyway, I think Romey's is a great name for a cafe bar. Sort of laid-back and sophisticated at the same time.

If this meal was anything to go by, Romey's should go like a bomb. My dad is a genius – coriander mushrooms, roast honey-glazed lamb with apricots and Persian rice; crème Brûlee. Afterwards we flopped out, too full to move. I lay on the rug, building towers of bricks with Romey. I built the towers and Romey whacked them down. He stared at the debris as if he couldn't believe his eyes, then he clapped his hands together and squealed, 'Dow! Dow!'

Dad and Jill were all snuggled up together on the settee. Dad had his hand on Jill's tummy. She's pregnant again. Already! She's got to get a move on, Mum says, because she doesn't have much time left. I tactfully turned my back and let them get on with it while I piled up bricks for Romey and let my mind drift back to last night.

'I think this young man should go out,' said Jill after a long while. 'Anyone up for a walk? Duck pond and swings? Swings and bandstand? Bandstand and canal?'

Dad had more or less melted into the settee. His eyes were closed. He groaned. Loudly. 'I remember when I looked forward to Sunday afternoons all week. Leisurely lunch. Bottle of wine. Bit of footie. Kip.'

Jill laughed and poked him in the ribs. 'You know you love it. I'll just go and get him dressed. Ten minutes, OK?'

'Hey! Look at this!' Dad was pretending he had actually been reading the paper that was scattered in bits all over the settee and the floor. 'A Paki from round here's gone and got himself beaten up.'

Jill's eyebrows shot to the ceiling. 'Peter! Don't you dare use that language in front of Romey.'

Dad looked shifty. 'Poor kid's had a real hammering! He's not one of your mates, is he, Caryn? Here, they've got his picture.' He thrust a wodge of newspaper under my nose. I should have known then, when I reached out to take it. I should have known that if Kobir was in the posh Sundays things would never be the same again.

The picture said it all! I heard myself gasp when I saw it! I had to take the paper over to the window so Dad couldn't see my face.

Kobir's head was encased in a helmet of dressings as thick my thumb. Smooth, round and white, it made me think of a button mushroom. Soft. Vulnerable. Crushable. Pipes and tubes looped around him. I couldn't see the monitors flashing their messages, but I knew they were there.

Beneath the whiteness of the bandages, his face was a dark blur – a mashed, lopsided, pulpy mess. Nothing was right and in its place. His closed eyes bulged out of their sockets, as smooth as eggs. One cheek was puffed up as big as a fist. His nose was splayed out to one side. His skin a lattice of stitching. Top and bottom lips were so swollen they no longer met in the middle. They looked as if they came from different mouths. The skin of his lower lip was stretched so tight it was nearly bursting. It glistened where it caught the light. His whole face was twisted, distorted; it looked like someone had taken hold of the top of his head and screwed it round, away from the bottom – so that the two halves no longer matched up.

The paper fell from my hands. I stared out of the window. The sky was all kinds of grey. Nearly purple over Stratford. The colour of a bruise. My stomach screwed itself up into a tight ball – as if it wanted to find somewhere to hide.

I wasn't ready for this. Not one little bit. I seriously thought Kobir would be on the mend by now. Sitting up in bed, with bandages and a drip, yes, but talking – chatting away to his mates. Cheeking the nurses. Having a laugh. So the *Gazette* had said 'head injuries'. It had also said 'being treated'. It had said 'serious' but it had said 'being treated'. And if 'being treated' didn't mean getting better, what did it mean?

Maybe it wasn't as bad as it looked. It was only a picture. All those tubes and pipes, all that shiny steel made it look worse than it was. He could wake up tomorrow. He could be OK tomorrow. I picked the paper up off the floor and this time I read the headline. I hadn't taken it in at first. I'd seen it, but I hadn't taken it in.

Coma Boy Fights For Life

Out of the window I could see down on to the canal. The sun had burst through the clouds and the dark grey water had a metallic gleam. The wind was getting up and ruffling the surface into little pleats. You could make a good jacket out of it.

On the other side of the water were the gardens of the houses which backed on to the towpath. Two little kids had their bikes out in one of the gardens and were riding round the paths. Then the littlest kid fell off. He didn't get up, he just lay there on the ground yelling his head off. A man came rushing out of the house and the little kid pointed at the big one and carried on yelling. He was saying, 'He pushed me!' It was almost as if I could hear him – as if I was right there in the garden with him and not in our room at all.

My eyes slid over the rest of the article. It didn't tell me anything I didn't know already. Kobir was badly hurt. He wasn't going to get better tomorrow. It was going to take time.

I chucked the paper back at Dad. 'I don't know him,' I said. 'I haven't even seen him around.'

Dad had sunk back into the sofa. His hands were clasped over his belly and he was twirling one thumb round the other one. 'Police are going to have their work cut out,' he said. 'No one round here's going to grass. Not for some Paki.'

5
ROGUE AERO

It's four in the morning. I'm awake. Again! I can't keep still. My body thrashes. My arms and legs twitch and jerk as if my finger is jammed in the light socket. The duvet has knotted itself round my legs. My sheet is twisted rope. I get up and stagger downstairs to make a cup of tea.

Hibiscus and deadnettle or elderflower and fennel? Davina again. Well why not? I put a teabag in the cup and cover it with boiling water and, because I've got nothing better to do, I watch to see what happens. Deep red hibiscus tea lies on the bottom of the cup with clear water on top of it. As separate as the blue and white stripes on the outside of the mug. Then, slowly, the red hibiscus begins to bleed into the clear water in loops and swirls.

BLEED. There's a click inside my head and there it is again – the face in the picture. Kobir's face. But he is not in hospital and there are no bandages on his head. He is on Canal Road. The face is battered, twisted, pulpy – but the eyes are open. Blood mats his hair. Blood courses down his face, over his eyes. His eyes are still open and he is looking straight at me through the blood that streams down over his eyes.

*

Mum clattered downstairs in her black work suit, stuck a slice of wholemeal in the toaster and grabbed her make-up bag. She keeps it in the cupboard behind the cereals and she can do foundation, eyeshadow and mascara in the time it takes to do one slice. Then she raced round, sorting her things for the office and packing them into her bag. I tipped a carton of black cherry yoghurt on to my cornflakes and shovelled them into my face while I drifted round, picking up my school stuff. I couldn't stop yawning. I was so tired I felt like I was wading through deep water. We kept knocking into each other and saying 'sorry'. She had to have a go at conversation all the same.

'I was horrified by that article in the paper about the poor boy who was beaten up on Friday. He's not anyone you know, is he, Caryn?'

'No,' I said. 'He goes to Joan Littlewood.' As if that settled it.

'I hope they find the animals who did it, but I don't suppose they will. People round here won't come forward. Too afraid of what the neighbours will say. Do you think they are part of an organized gang, or do you think it was just an isolated incident?'

'Mum!' I snapped. 'It could have been the Spiders from Mars for all I know.'

Mum's eyebrows shot up. 'All right, Caryn! Sorry I spoke! Anyway, if you're in tonight, I'll be here. I've got some sweaters to wash.'

Oh. Right. Sweaters. Thanks a lot, Mum. 'I'm going out,' I said. 'I'll be at Layla's.'

Mum's question had got me going though. Were

Kobir's attackers an organized gang, or were they just a bunch of low-life tossers who had got together in the pub? And if they were a gang, what else did they get up to? What were they going to do next? I felt another click coming on. A kind of pressure above my left eye. Well, I wasn't hanging round to find out what it was about this time! I was away over the road and on to the Fields opposite our house, running, running – until the only pressure I could feel was my lungs gasping for air. Mango looped in circles round me, barking and yipping for joy.

School was mental! Now Kobir's picture had been in the papers, everyone wanted to be in on the action. Everyone knew someone who knew him. Or his brother. Or his cousin. Roderick Quayle had played football with someone who had played against Kobir's team. Sabrina Smith knew someone who was at infant school with his sister. Some of the Bengalis must have known him because they all know each other, but a lot of them had stayed away and the rest were keeping themselves to themselves in a corner of the yard.

Questions flew from group to group. Which gang did it? Was it Jason and Garys' brother Nathan's? Or Phil's, who left last year? Were they Bethnal Green or were they Bow? Or had they come from Stratford? Or the Island?

Jason and Gary Cook and their mates in 11K turned up to school. Jason hasn't set foot inside the gates for six months. They staked out the corner by the shed and waited for trouble to start – and when it didn't, they drifted away again. If anyone said anything to them, what they said was, 'Yeah? Is that right? Don't know nothing about that. I wasn't there.' Which was meant to mean, 'I was there.' But was probably a lie.

Kendra's voice punched along the corridor towards me – forty decibels, with a shrill fizz of rage on top. Then I saw her stripe of golden hair in the middle of a crowd that had gathered round the Coke machine. She was sounding off at Larraine – which was not unusual: they loathe each other's guts. Kendra's finger was jabbing at Larraine's face so close it looked like her nail was going to take a slice out of her cheek.

'You what? Say that again! Say that again! Go on!'

Natalie was hauling at her arm. 'Leave it, Kendra,' she was saying. 'Don't take any notice. She's just ignorant, that's all.'

She could have been trying to tug the *Titanic* off the iceberg. Kendra didn't even know she was there.

'I don't believe I'm hearing this,' she shouted. 'The kid is in hospital. He's in a coma. For all we know he could be dying. And you stand there and say that.'

Larraine's mates slithered up close, one each side, until they were just touching her.

'All I said was that maybe this is what it takes to get it across to them that they're not wanted here,' she said. 'That they'd be better off going home.' When she began to speak she poked her head forward, slowly, and when she had finished she drew it back again. Like a tortoise poking its head in and out of its shell.

Kendra surged forward. 'All you said! Oh, is that all you said ...? So who's "them"? Who do you call "them" then? My mum's granddad came from Trinidad. He married my great grandnan in Cardiff. Does that make me "them"?'

'Kendra, forget it!' I said, grabbing the other arm. 'It's not worth it.'

Larraine had screwed herself up tight behind her folded arms, but she didn't back down. 'You know who I mean,' she said. 'You all know who I mean. You just pretend you don't. And deep down you think the same, only you won't admit it. You think you're so clever.'

Kendra was swollen up with rage, I swear. Her mouth was open and her eyes were popping out of her head. She looked like she was going to burst. Then her arm went back and up. 'Don't you dare tell me what I think . . .'

'Girls! Girls!' Doherty's voice arrived a long time before she did. She shoved her way through the crowd and planted herself between Larraine and Kendra. 'Easy! Take it easy now! Time to go to your classrooms. Kendra, calm down. We don't want any trouble now, do we?'

'You never heard what she said, miss! I can't let her get away with that!' Kendra was hopping from one foot to another and her arms jerked uselessly in Larraine's direction.

'Kendra, what is your next lesson? Art? Well, get along to the artroom. Now! Not later! I want to see you move! And Larraine, you too. Get to your classroom.'

Doherty had the situation under control – just. Kendra stomped off down the corridor, throwing furious glances over her shoulder at Larraine's back.

I linked my arm through Natalie's and we went off to our lesson. Nat was upset too. Her back was as stiff as a board and she clamped my arm to her skinny ribs so hard I couldn't pull it free.

'Kendra really goes for it, doesn't she?' I said. 'She doesn't care.'

'Yeah and doesn't she just love it!' snorted Natalie. 'She's gotta to be right in there, shooting her mouth off. She really gets off on it!'

'Natalie!' I was gobsmacked. 'That's a terrible thing to say! You know what Kendra's like. She can't stand to see anyone getting pushed around. She'd stick up for anybody. You know she would. You're supposed to be her mate after all!'

Natalie's neck was bright red, and pink splodges were spattered across her face. Her eyes looked bright and glassy.

'You think so?' she said. 'I think she's loving it, just like the rest of them.'

'Nat! I can't believe I'm hearing this! Kendra cares. And I care. I want Kobir to get better. I do!'

Natalie raked her hair off her face so she could look me in the eye. 'You, Caryn? Pakis get beaten up all the time. What's so special about this one?'

I couldn't wait to see Layla after school. I'd phoned her first thing Sunday to tell her about Craig and me, and she had made me go over every single detail. But I got a text later, at Dad's: '**U lied 2 me.**' Lied? What was she on about? All she'd say was, 'I'm not discussing it on the phone.'

Layla was still at college when I got to her house, so I sat in the garden with Bridget, who was busy working on her vine. I was there when she planted it, and now it grows right across the end of the garden, from one wall to the other. Underneath is a cool green cave, where the whole family sit out in summer. Bunches of grapes hung down from the branches, and Bridget moved between them, feeling the weight of one, then another, in her hand.

'You looking forward to the party Saturday?' she said. 'Ari's party?'

She didn't have to ask. Ari was Layla's brother and Saturday was his eighteenth. There was going to be a big family dinner and then a party for Ari's mates at the house he shares with other students in Stratford. I was going to both.

'I can't wait,' I said. 'It's going to be a great evening! I'm bringing a friend, if that's OK?'

Bridget smiled. 'You bring him along and let us all have a good look at him.'

Bridget's smile changes her whole face. Her cheeks bunch and push her eyes up at the corners until they are just slanty lines with beads of light in the middle. She is the most unstressed person I know. It must be because she's so old. She was older than Mum is now when Layla was born!

The front door slammed and I could hear Layla moving about inside the house. As soon as she showed her face at the back door I could see she had the hump. She strode down the garden towards me, grabbed me by the hand and pulled me to my feet.

'I need to speak to Caryn, Mum. It's private,' she said, and dragged me back into the house.

In the kitchen, the kettle was boiling. Layla made us coffee in silence, piled biscuits on to a plate and carried them upstairs. I followed her. I wasn't saying anything: she started this. In her room, I helped myself to biscuits, kicked off my shoes and jumped on to the bed. Layla and me always sit on her bed to talk. She still made me wait, though, while she pulled off her scrunchy and shook out her hair.

'You lied to me!' she said. 'You said that you had seen someone being beaten up. That was a lie!'

'Layla!' I was gobsmacked. 'I told you I saw Kobir – that kid who was in the papers . . .'

'And it was a blatant lie!' Layla interrupted. 'You said, "I saw someone being beaten up yesterday." You never said, "I saw a kid being just about killed." You never said, "He was being battered by a bunch of racist scum." You never said, "There was blood all over the road." What you said was a lie. It must be a lie, because it definitely is not the truth.'

'Layla,' I said. 'I tried to tell you. You didn't want to listen. You just wanted to get to Roxanne's.'

Layla gave my leg a slap. Hard. It stung. 'I'm serious,' she said. 'Something's wrong. You don't lie. Not to me, anyway. Something must be wrong or you would have told me about it properly. But you're going to tell me everything now. And I mean it – right! Every single thing!'

So I told her. The whole story. About the white transit . . . the figure on the ground . . . the vermin slamming into it with their boots . . . how I hurried by . . . and then turned.

'You what!' Layla shrieked. 'I don't believe I'm hearing this! You're outa there and you turn round! What, were you right off your head?'

Then I told her about Rosie. Standing alone, away from the action. I could see it now. He was the leader of the pack, all right. There was a connection between him and them like an invisible wire. When he turned his face away from them and looked straight at me up on the bridge, the kicking eased right off. They were doing it for him. They needed him to see it.

Layla and I were facing each other on the bed now. My head was almost touching hers and she was gripping my feet, her thumbs digging hard into the soles. 'Whaddya do then?'

I told her how I flew over the bridge to Martineau Street, and about Rosie chasing me, and fixing me to the pavement with his crazy, screw-ball eyes.

'And I just stood there,' I said. 'Like a dummy.'

'Why didn't you just run away? There's shops on Martineau Street. You could have run into a shop.' Layla was bouncing up and down in frustration now, and the mattress bounced too.

Why? How to explain that I couldn't move? That my legs had stopped working. That something had happened to the wiring between muscles and brain. 'D'you remember when Dad and I went to Wales in Uncle Al's camper van? We stayed on a farm right up in the hills. Miles from anywhere. One evening we're walking up to the farm to get some eggs, and there they are, on the path in front of us, a tortoiseshell cat and a rabbit. They're frozen like statues – their eyes locked – their noses almost touching. We stand and watch but they don't move a muscle, either of them. They can't. If the rabbit moves – the cat springs. The cat moves – the rabbit is off.'

'He's the cat!' gasped Layla.

'And I'm the rabbit,' I said. 'If I move, what's he going to do? Let me go? I don't think so. He's going to jump.'

'Did he say anything?' said Layla, the fingers of both hands netting her mouth.

'He didn't have to,' I said. 'I knew what he was saying. And he knew I knew.'

6
ratty pest

'Needle noodle?' A tiny Chinese gentleman in a robe the colour of wet ink looked up at me. His eyebrows finished the question for him. We don't get many Chinese; they have their own shops, but we do have a shelf full of noodles. I was showing him where they were when Warwick and his mate Ezra bundled in. Warwick was hanging his whole weight on Ezra's arm and grabbing for the large brown envelope that Ezra flapped above his head.

'Hey! June, man. Get a look at this. You ain't gonna believe it.' The envelope crackled as Ezra flourished it in the air.

'Stop messin', Ez! Give 'em to me. You'll spoil 'em.' Warwick gave a desperate leap, got his hands on the envelope and smoothed it down against his belly.

June heard the noise from the back of the shop. 'Wappen bwoy? What al de nise?'

Ezra had hardly noticed the envelope had gone. 'Wappen!' he squeaked. 'The *Gazette* only buyed three of his pictures! Not one! Three! And! And! They arks him for more work! They rate him, man! They rate him!'

'That right, son?' said June.

Warwick was fighting to hang on to his cool. His

mouth was stretching at the corners, in–out, in–out, like an elastic band, and his eyes were dancing, flashing light around like sparklers.

'The *Gazette* has accepted three of my pictures,' he said stiffly, 'and they would like me to submit more of my work.' And his face just exploded into a massive grin.

June grinned too. 'You be earnin' now then? Wi'dat toy you got? You be earnin' good money?'

Warwick was saying, 'I ain't in this for the money, Dad,' but no one was listening. June threw five, Warwick caught, only a second late, and they danced around in the tiny space in front of the counter. Ezra clapped them both on the back and leaped up and down in circles around them, his locks whipping his face.

I leaped up and down on my spot behind the counter and clapped my hands too because I was pleased for Warwick, I really was.

The Chinaman hadn't budged an inch. As soon as things calmed down, I found him his noodles and he bowed till his head nearly touched the floor. Then he left the shop.

'Catch you later then,' said Warwick. 'I got work to do.'

'Not for much longer, ay?' said Ezra, grinning. 'You soon be outa here for good! Mr Photographer!'

'Let's see them then,' I said, when Ezra had gone.

'See what?' said Warwick, back to his usual self.

'Your pictures, of course!'

'You seen my pictures before. You never said nothing then.' He had to moan, but he handed the envelope over.

There were pictures of Olly and Ezra together. Just their heads against a white wall. Looking away from each other, the light catching their cheekbones. And people in the street. Traders. Tramps. Kids hanging out. And a nice one, through a window at night, of a couple of guys boxing, silhouetted against a blind.

'Which one is going in the *Gazette*?' I asked. I didn't have to wait for an answer. I had it in my hand.

It was a picture of the mad gun shop in Miranda Street. The usual lethal-looking stuff – knives, pistols, rifles, ammunition – is all neatly laid out in rows on an old Union Jack flag. But there is something new that I haven't seen before. A big gun, like a machine gun, stands on its own in the middle of the window. It is pointing straight into a group of dollies. Grown-up dollies, all done up in frills and lace, their blonde hair puffed up into *Dynasty*-style whirls. Their dumb made-up faces stare straight down the barrel of the gun – they are about to be wasted and they don't even know it.

What was that about? It was weird! Horrible! But it was a brilliant picture! I turned round to tell Warwick . . .

'Excuse me. When you're quite ready.' A yuppie from the posh flats they've squeezed into a corner of the Bijoya School playground thrust a packet under my nose.

'How am I supposed to know if this is Egyptian or Turkish saffron when the writing's not in English?'

Her voice sawed away at me, but she had a point. I shouted for Warwick. She turned her head away and gazed out through the window, as if looking at me was more than she could be expected to endure.

Warwick bustled back to the till. 'Yes, madam, I can assure you it is genuine Egyptian saffron. Is there anything further you require?'

'I don't suppose you stock the *FT*?' said pink shirt and red braces who was with her.

'Certainly, sir,' said Warwick. 'And anything else you want we can order.'

'Is there anything further you require?' I said, when they had gone, taking him off. 'You even walk different for customers like her.'

'That's right. It's my obsequious walk. And it works!'

'You grovelling git!'

'No. That's where you're wrong. I ain't grovelling to no one. I'm just showing awareness of the customer-retailer relationship. Them yuppies come here in droves. They don't go to Momtaz Mini-Mart and they don't go to Les's.'

'Well, I'm not grovelling to no one, all right?'

'Yeah. Right. Whatever,' said Warwick. 'Are you coming to the vigil tomorrow evening?'

VIGIL. The word screamed a warning inside my head like the bell for fire drill. Of course I knew what it was about – it didn't take two brains after all – but I wasn't letting on. Warwick was trying to slide it past me. He does it all the time – slips things he wants me to do into a conversation about something else. He thinks I'll say yes without even noticing. That is truly what he thinks of my intellect.

'I don't have a clue what you're on about,' I said.

Warwick rolled out his patient look. 'There's a vigil for Kobir Chowdhury outside the London Hospital tomorrow evening. Seven o'clock. You should come.'

'I'm going out,' I said. 'I've got a date.'

'Come first,' said Warwick. 'It's at seven o'clock. You'll have time to go home and change. There'll be a few hundred people there, maybe more. There's people coming from all over East London. Press'll be there. We might even make the evening news on telly.'

'Why a vigil?' I asked. 'Kobir's OK. He's getting better. He'll be out of hospital soon.'

Warwick gave me a long look, then he said, 'Some of us want to let Kobir know we're there for him – and to support his family too. We'll be outside the hospital at dusk with candles. One or two people might say something, but mostly it's silent. We want to tell them that we don't all feel like those bastards who put him where he is.'

'Well it won't do Kobir much good, will it?' I said spitefully. 'He's in a coma in case you hadn't noticed. You're wasting your time.'

'Nobody knows what goes on in your head when you're in a coma,' said Warwick. 'Some of our energy might get through to him. You never know.'

'You don't really believe that,' I snapped. 'He's right out of it for the moment.'

'Whatever,' said Warwick. 'Anyway, I just think you should be there.'

Should! He was getting on my nerves. Who was Warwick to tell me what I should do? He might be my boss in the shop, but no way was he telling me what to do anywhere else.

'Leave it out, Warwick!' I shouted. 'I'm not interested, right. Kobir Chowdhury is not my problem. But you go. You should find some brilliant photo opportunities.' The words punched out at him. I'd just about had enough of him going on at me. 'Candlelight. Dusk. Grieving relatives. The *Gazette*'ll go mad for all that.'

That did it. He took a step back, arms out, fingers towards the ceiling. Protecting himself – from me.

'Just get off my case, Warwick,' I roller-coastered on. 'You go to this vigil thing if you want, but leave me right out, OK.'

'Fine, Caryn, you do what you want,' he spoke very quietly, 'but you can't hide away forever. You gonna have to face this thing sooner or later, you see!' And he turned his back on me and whisked away to the end of the shop.

I get home in a bad mood. The house is empty and cold. It's Mum's college night. She's catching up on the education she missed by having me.

The place is the usual Tuesday night tip – only worse. There's an overturned chair on the floor. You can't see the table for paper – mostly college stuff, but newspapers and a couple of catalogues as well. Dirty cups and plates on top of it all, the remains of what looks like beans on toast and fried egg.

Thanks, Mum!

My dog's not speaking to me. She's curled up in a tight ball under the sideboard, looking reproachfully at me through the feathery fur of her tail. She hates it when I work late even though I come home at lunchtime to give her a run – and she hates it even more when I stay at Layla's without her. I haul her out and shove her out of the front door and she's away over the Fields without a backward glance.

I clean up in the house and what happens is the cold, empty space moves inside me. It clings to my ribs crying out to be filled. I stick a family pack of chips in the oven and look for something to spice them up a bit. Garlic mayo! I tip half a bottle of gloop on to a plate where it shivers like wallpaper paste. Not what I need at all. Then I remember the salsa – Volcano Island Red Chilli Salsa that Warwick gave me for a bet. On the white plate it is pure flame. I feel the warmth creeping through my belly just looking at it. I call Mango in and we curl up on the sofa to eat. Mango adores chips and whimpers at me until I give her some, but they are too hot for her and she tosses her head like she's got a fly on the end of her nose.

Then somehow I get it into my head that the mayo is salsa and the salsa is mayo. I scoop up a handful of chips and wipe them round in the mayo to get them good and loaded – only it's not mayo, and even though I can see the chips are dripping orange, I shove the lot into my mouth – and I'm hopping round the room in agony, hands flapping, screaming blue murder. My mouth is on fire. The burn sears right down to my stomach. I think I'm going to die.

I race into the kitchen, fling open the freezer, rake out frozen snow with my fingers and cram it into my mouth until the cold hurts more than the heat. Tears stream down my face on to the snowball that sticks out of my mouth.

When the pain dies down my bad mood is gone with it, leaving me with a clear head. Why did I say what I did to Warwick about photo opportunities? It hurt him. He had to push me away. All right, I was fed up with him going on about the vigil, but all I had to do was say I wasn't going. I didn't have to do one like that, did I?

I rummage through the freezer for the tub of Cherry Garcia I hid at the back for emergencies and I eat it. All of it. When it's all gone I scrape the carton so hard that the spoon makes tracks in the waxy coating.

7

touch sad

The phone rang when I was in the shower. I knew instantly from the ring-tone that it wasn't good news. I can always tell.

'Caaa-ryn.' Craig's voice wheedled at me down the phone.

I knotted the towel more tightly around me. Red Colour-in-Rinse dripped down my back and blobbed on to the floor.

'I'm not going to be able to make tonight. Something's come up I can't do anything about. Sorry an' that. I do want to see you – but not tonight. All right?'

Something's come up! Something more important than me! I feel as if I'm falling – a Ramses Revenge drop on to jets of freezing spray. The ice is in my voice. 'Something, Craig? What does she look like, this something?'

'I know what it must sound like, but it isn't another girl, Caryn. I wouldn't do that to you. Christian rang me last night – he needs someone to help supervise the Dolphins cos Sean let him down. I gotta do it, Caryn. He can't find anyone else. But I want to see you, I do. I'm training Thursday so let's make it Friday – OK?'

Kendra would tell him to get lost, and that would be the end of it. There're no second chances with her. But Craig's no Romeo. I believed him when he said it wasn't another girl. There was a kind of edge to his voice that sounded like the truth.

'I'm going out Friday,' I said, which wasn't exactly a lie. I go out Fridays. 'There's a party Saturday. You can come if you want.'

I was going to go to school, but at half past nine I was laid out on the settee in front of the telly watching Kilroy mixing it with two lads who hadn't spoken to their dad for two years because his new partner told lies about them. He really got them going. They never see it. How he winds them up and gets them all arguing and yelling at each other. Then I got bored of that so I switched over channels.

'I'll just have one more coffee,' I said to Mango, 'and then I'm off.' But I watched *This Morning* right through till twelve o'clock. Craig's phone call had really dragged me down.

That, and the fact I just couldn't face school. I wasn't the only one either. Yesterday, empty chairs dotted the classrooms. The atmosphere had turned really bad. Insults hissed along the corridors. Scuffles started in the playground and developed into real fights outside the school gates. Snappy, strung-out teachers, who had been kicked out of the staff room, picked on anything that moved.

'Come on, girl!' I called to Mango, grabbing her lead from the hook. She couldn't believe her luck and hurled herself out of the door before I could change my mind. I drifted over to my seat in the middle of the Fields. It's where I come to think. Beyond the crumpled blocks of flats piled along the edges like old cereal boxes, I could see the steel and glass towers of the city. The morning sun was going supernova in the glass walls. I sat and looked at all that dazzle and energy thrusting itself up into the sky and I felt light and easy. No pressure. That's what I wanted. No pressure.

Right by me, a woman crusty was doing T'ai chi. Her dog was tied to my seat on a long piece of string. She wore baggy trousers and a brightly striped waistcoat from Tibet, and her hair was plaited with coloured cottons. I could see people were saying things about her, but she didn't notice; she just kept on making weird movements with her hands and looking at the sky.

Mango was an orange streak in the distance, racing round in circles with another dog. I hollered her name and she came reluctantly to heel. I didn't have any plans. You don't bunk school to make plans. Maybe the market to check out Shuja's knock-offs and Alomgir's cut-price CDs? Or the leather jackets on Bethnal Green Road and a salmon and cream cheese bagel and baked sultana cheesecake in Brick Lane? Or just a run with Mango and a stretch out on the settee with a couple of Warwick's videos? Maybe. No pressure. But the pressure caught up with me.

The graffiti wall is not exactly on the way to Brick Lane, but it's always worth a look. It runs alongside the hole where the Central Line disappears into the ground. Five hundred yards of tags and stuff – **Dappa D** – **Fish and Faz** – **Dummy Gang** – **Respect de Bridge Boys** – **Leli is Fit**. But down by the car park it changes. It gets serious. Or just mental. **Stephanie Crisis Death** – **Dave Parker, you bastard, you have a little girl** – **Nicco, I'll find you one day**.

Then I saw one that cracked me up, right next to the phone box, in purple letters a foot high – **Kenn Dodds Dadds Doggs Deadd**. What was that about? What was it meant to mean? Maybe it was just there to get a laugh. I crossed over the road to get a closer look, and then, as I stared, other words began to grin through from underneath. Faded. Patchy. Almost obliterated by layers of paint. **Gary Davis is a Grass!**

The noise comes at me from all sides! From the air. From the walls. From the pavement underneath my feet. A clacking, juddering roar! Cringing into the side of a parked car, I make myself look up. A monstrous yellow bird fills the sky . . .

I blink – and I'm back in reality – the yellow ambulance helicopter hovers, then drops on to the helipad on the roof of the London Hospital.

Mango! An empty collar dangles from the lead in my hand. No sign of her up and down the street. I call her name, shout her name, scream her name. Nothing! I throw myself to the ground and peer underneath the line of parked cars. No dog! At the first deafening burst from the helicopter she must have taken off. She's got a bit of greyhound in her the way she runs; terrified, she'd be greased lightning.

I ran on in the direction we had been walking when the noise came, shouting her name. No Mango! No sign of her at the T-junction either. My heart was pounding. A hundred yards away I could see the main road, a six-lane highway of speed-crazed, maniac trucks and cars. If she'd shot straight out of a side road and under a truck, I had to know. It would kill me. I would just die right there, on the spot – but I had to know. Then all feeling left me; it poured out of me like water out of a cup and I sprinted towards the intersection.

No dog. But no relief. There were other intersections on the main road. I got some very funny looks as I wove in and out of the crowds, shouting, 'Mango! Mango! Mango!' One daft pillock shouted back, 'Banana! Banana!', but I didn't have time to deal with him. I gave him the finger and ran on.

I found her two blocks away by the wet fish stall, where she had come to a stop. A big, purple-faced man in a white apron was throwing her frozen prawns.

'Your dog?' he asked, which wasn't strictly necessary as Mango was practically airborne with delight, licking my face and whining. 'What you bin doing to her?' he demanded, shoving his face up close to mine. 'Poor thing's terrified. Trembling like a leaf, she was. Good job I found her.'

I had to thank him. It was his stall that stopped her. 'She was frightened by the helicopter,' I replied. 'Thank you for the prawns.'

'That's all right,' he said, melting a little. 'It's just I can't stand cruelty to animals. Makes me mad.'

I dragged her over to the almshouses gate, collapsed on to the step and hugged and hugged her. 'Daft dog, daft dog, I love you daft dog.' Then I started to cry. I must have looked a sight: tear-stained, clothes gritty from lying on the pavement. I wiped my face in the silky fur on Mango's neck, and brushed myself down as well as I could.

The helicopter squatted on the roof of the hospital just over the road. The hospital, where Mango's headlong flight had brought us. The hospital where Kobir was fighting for his life. The last place on the planet that I wanted to be.

Hundreds of years of passing feet had made a bum-shaped depression in the step I was sitting on. I rested my hand on the stone; it was warm in the sun. Under my fingertips I could feel some of the trillions of grains of sand and sea creatures that made it. I must have sat there for ages, looking across at the hospital windows.

'Come on, Kobir,' I whispered. 'You can make it. You can!'

8

CURVE DEVIL

Kendra had been at the vigil. Of course she had. And she was buzzing with it. She slid up to me in the Study Centre and hissed into my ear, 'Caryn, it was ama-azing! You never seen nothing like it! There must have been hundreds there, but it was dead quiet. No one said a word. We was all stood there, holding our candles up to the window – the window where he was. It was like being in church. I'm telling you, it makes me feel funny inside just thinking about it. You shoulda been there. It was brilliant. You'da loved it!'

She was wriggling and twisting herself in knots as she spoke, like the feelings inside her were so strong she couldn't keep still. Then she shut up and gazed out of the window with wide, shining eyes. Looking at her, I could see what Natalie was getting at. You poser, I thought. That's not real. You're just trying to impress yourself. Then I thought, shut up, Caryn. That's horrible. Kendra's your mate.

Kendra must have been at a different vigil from the rest of the school. Everyone else was talking fight-fight-fight and nothing else. The peaceful scene outside Kobir's window didn't last long. A gang in black balaclavas ripped in from nowhere to break it up. And enough guys were ready for them. All from our school, if you believe it. Mujibur Rahman had to have nine stitches in his head. Abdul Mukith pulled one of the gang off Aidan Coughlin and saved his life. Chantelle Abbot grabbed a baseball bat off the guy who was beating up her boyfriend and knocked him unconscious. Iqubal Hussain and Motosir Rahman were dragged off to the cells – and they swore they had to stay there till morning because the police took away their trousers.

It was doing my head in! By lunchtime, I couldn't take any more and I went to find Natalie. She was in the office, photocopying for Mrs Olubusola. The machine was clunk-clunking along by itself and Natalie was standing in her Kate Moss pose, in a trance. She'd done her hair in a different way – in twists, pinned away from her face with pink and mauve butterflies. It must have taken ages! Every single other person in school is rushing to get in for all the goss, and Nutty Natalie is twisting her hair, strand by strand, and fixing it with a crown of plastic butterflies!

She didn't give a toss about the vigil. It all happened light years away, as far as she was concerned, in a different solar system and didn't touch her at all. But when I shouted, 'I gotta get outa here! You coming, Nat?' she nodded, slipped her arms into the sleeves of her leather jacket and followed me.

We were nearly out of the gate when Kendra's voice peeled across the playground, 'Hey! Where d'you two think you're goin'? Wait for me!' She caught us up, grabbed Natalie's arm and shook it. 'What's goin' on? You were goin' off without me!'

'Actually,' said Natalie, 'we didn't think you'd want to come with us. We're too boring! We stayed in last night and watched *EastEnders*! We didn't go to no poxy vigil!' She tossed her hair back over her shoulder while she spoke so that her face turned right away from Kendra.

'Me and Nat need to get outa here,' I said. 'And you're really into talking about last night. We didn't think you'd want to come.'

'And we're not into talking about last night,' said Natalie. 'We're fed up to the back teeth with last night. We're going to puke up all over anyone who even mentions last night!'

We bought a family size box of chicken nuggets and took them down to the canal lock to eat them. It's peaceful down there. They've made a little park with benches and tubs of geraniums. There's even a kind of waterfall. A side channel tumbles down over a sloping stone into the main canal. It makes me want to laugh when I look at it because it doesn't look like water. With the sun on it, it looks just like the stone is covered in bubble wrap. I stretch myself out on the bench and begin to relax.

Natalie was going on and on about Craig – telling me how to run my life. I wasn't really listening. I don't always listen to Natalie. Just because she has been going out with Reuben forever she thinks she knows everything there is to know about boys. I tune out – like I was doing now. Kendra was sitting on the edge of the lock, her legs dangling over the water, chucking stones at the lock gates. Hard. They thwacked angrily into the wood. She hadn't said much since we left school, which is not like her at all. She is always mouthing off about one thing or another. I couldn't see her face, but her back was saying that she was in a bad mood.

'He's got to take you somewhere really nice where you can dress up – Mood or Ignight are good. You mustn't let him get away with . . .' Natalie was saying.

Kendra swung her legs up to ground level and hopped over to where we were sitting. 'You shoulda seen her face,' she said. 'You shoulda seen her face when they threw the stone.' Her voice sounded fuzzy – like only half of it was there and the rest had got lost on the way out.

Natalie blanked her. She carried on talking exactly as if Kendra hadn't spoken, '. . . nights down the pub with his mates,' she said. 'If you let them get away with it once they'll do it all the time. You gotta . . .'

Kendra goes, 'Someone threw a stone at his mum, would you believe? I thought she was going to burst into tears. But she didn't. She held on to the mike and she carried on talking.'

'Kobir's mum?' I said. I missed a beat. 'I didn't know his mum was there.'

'His mum was there,' goes Kendra, 'speaking from a platform. She was speaking when the scum came in from the back . . .'

'Did the stone hit her?' I asked.

Natalie gave me a 'Whose side are you on?' look. Deep pink colour was beginning to creep across her chest in a jagged line – it looked as if she was wearing a pink lace top. 'Caryn!' she squeaks. 'Are you listening to me. What I'm telling you is important. You gotta . . .'

What was going on? I'd asked Natalie to come down here to get away from all the talk about the vigil, and what was I doing? Talking about the vigil. So his mum was there? She could be there if she wanted. It didn't make it any different because his mum was there.

It was different all right. If his mum was there, speaking into a mike from a platform . . . it was different, that's all.

'Who else was there?' I asked.

'Loads of people,' said Kendra. 'Lots of his family . . .'

'Kendra!' squawked Natalie. 'Will you shut up about your poxy vigil. We don't want to hear it, right! I don't know why you went in the first place. It's got nothing to do with you!'

'Excuse me! Ex-cuse me!' Kendra was on her feet now. 'I only live here, don't I? And there's things happening right here – right where I live! Are you saying I shouldn't care about that? About things that could have happened to me? Or any of my mates? And I wanted to see what's goin' on for myself. You got a problem with that?'

'Don't lie!' Natalie was on her feet too. Her arm sliced at the air, underlining every word. 'Nothing's gonna happen to you and you know it! You went cos you always have to be part of the action. You always have to be right in the middle of anything that's going on. And you get off on trouble – just like everybody else. You were dissing Kobir and his family. You didn't go for them at all, you went for the buzz!'

Kendra didn't say a word. Her mouth was hanging open as if she couldn't find the words to put in it!

I said, 'That is so not true, Nat. Kendra was gutted about the fight, I know she was!' Neither of them took a blind bit of notice of me.

'Well I hate it,' shouted Natalie. 'I hate the way everybody goes looking for trouble, and gets off on it, and pretends they're there for some poor kid who is lying there in a coma – and no one says anything about that at all.'

Natalie and Kendra both looked as if they didn't know what had hit them. Natalie's face was covered in pink blotches. Their eyes were locked on to each other, and the tension between them was so strong I could have reached out and pinged it.

On the other side of the canal they've built new flats, ten storeys high with pointy metal balconies that are meant to make you think of boats. Squeezed in-between them is a small square house. The lock keeper's cottage. Two storeys high, made of big square stone blocks like the lock, it looked strong and neat and safe – like a money box. I wanted to climb inside it and pull the lid shut on top of me, away from all this grief.

'Look at the cottage,' I said. 'D'you think it's lonely, stuck there with no houses of its own age to talk to?'

The thread that was holding them together snapped. Then both of them turned on me. If that was what I wanted to happen, it had worked.

'Caryn!' shouted Kendra. 'What crap are you on about now? Have you gone right off your head? We're talking serious stuff here.'

'What are you like, Caryn!' Natalie scolded. 'It's a house. A house doesn't have feelings. And you're not four years old any more. That's the stupidest thing I've ever heard!' She turned to Kendra. 'Anyway! I'm fed up with this place. I'm going back to school.'

She ran off along the towpath towards the road, which goes to show how upset she was. Natalie hasn't run since she was seven because everyone laughs at her when she does.

'That's right! Run away, why don't you!' Kendra yelled after her. She turned to me. 'Why's she being like this, Caryn? Somebody tell me what's going on? What's happening to her and me?' Then she turned and sprinted off along the towpath after Natalie.

I didn't know. Natalie and Kendra had been best mates ever since their mums had done their breathing exercises together at antenatal class. They saw eye to eye about everything. I'd never, ever seen them fight. And now something was coming between them. It had something to do with what had happened to Kobir, but I couldn't put my finger on what it was. Not at all.

I walked over to the edge of the lock. It was a long way down to the water. Curtains of green slime hung from the walls. Rubbish had collected in the corners by the gates. I almost gagged on the mud smell. I chucked the empty chicken nugget packet in and walked back to school.

I was sprawled out on the floor in front of the telly when Mum bounced in with a soaking wet Mango, who was banished to the kitchen before she could shake herself all over me. Mum's hair was dripping and her face was flushed and shiny with water.

I'm about to say something friendly like, 'Is it raining out then?' but she takes one look at me and starts, 'Caryn, what are you doing? It's a school day. Haven't you got any homework?'

I'm ready for it. 'This is homework,' I say. '"The Concept of White in Advertising". I'm waiting for the ads to come on.' I wave my notebook under her nose to prove it.

It doesn't work. She shakes some water off her hair, takes a couple of deep breaths – and we're off! The lecture! Yes, that lecture. The one I've heard at least once a week since I was twelve years old. The words she speaks match themselves to the words already inside my head – words I've heard over and over: 'never listened . . . left at sixteen . . . no O levels . . . crazy gear . . . make-up . . . bands . . . all over the country . . . PREGNANT.' There's no escape. I'm stuck with it until I get a full house.

My mum was a punk. You'd never think so to look at her now, but she was. There's a picture of her with pink spiked-up hair, rings in her ears, rings through her nose and black lines round her eyes that make her look like Queen Nefertiti. They wouldn't allow her to come to school like that so she left, and went around the country in Dad's van following bands. Siousxie and the Banshees. The Jam. The Clash. The Raincoats. Then she fell pregnant. Or ruined her life as she puts it now! And she's terrified I'll do the same.

I know not to interrupt. Let her get on with it, get it out of her system, and what happens is she runs out of steam. When that happens she can be in quite a good mood. And when she had finished, she was.

She jumped on to the sofa and flopped down with her legs crossed in front of her. 'There I go again. Sorry, love. Change the record, ay?'

She still looks quite good when she isn't exhausted and stressed out. She'd changed her work suit for T-shirt and track-pants which are her type of clothes. She'd even put on lipstick, which was a good sign – even if it is seaside rock pink and most of it has come off in the rain.

'Hey, Caryn,' she patted the seat beside her. 'What about a takeaway and a bottle of wine? We haven't had one for ages. Then you can tell me all about this new course. What do you fancy? Chinese? Indian? Thai?'

I go 'Thai' before she can change her mind. I've only ever had Thai once and, as far as I'm concerned, it doesn't get any better than that.

Geng Ped, Pat Pahk, Tod Man Pla – neither of us had a clue what to order. We were giggling away outside the takeaway, with rain streaming down our faces and soaking our hair. We must have looked like a couple of lunatics.

I ended up with little meaty parcels in soup, and vegetables cooked with chilli and lemon rice. The soup wasn't like any soup I had ever tasted. White, creamy with coconut and packed with weird bits – it was gorgeous.

It is so good and so strange that I pick little pieces up from my bowl and put them in my mouth one by one so I only get one flavour at a time. I don't want to muddle things up yet. It cracks Mum up.

'You always did that when you were little,' she says, laughing. 'Ate one thing at a time – all your peas first, then your chips, then fish fingers last. If I mixed your food up, you yelled and threw it on the floor.'

I rummage about a bit and pull out something that looks like a little woody star and tastes of aniseed. Then, at the bottom of my bowl, there's something else that looks like a piece of stick that has got in by mistake. I'm about to throw it out, but I shove it in my mouth first, in case. It tastes of lemon, sour lemon plus lemon.

'Mum, what is it?' I say.

Mum is pouring herself another glass of wine. It's her fourth. I haven't finished my first yet.

'Come on, Caryn. As if I'd know. Ask your dad. He's the cook. The only thing I know about Thai food is lemon grass.'

Grass! That word! I'm like, 'Mum, have you heard of someone called Gary Davis?'

Mum looked thoughtful. 'It rings a bell. Why? Who is he?'

'I don't know. It's a name I keep seeing on walls and stuff.'

'What, "Gary Davis is innocent!"? I haven't seen one of those for a long time. They used to be everywhere. You know, where you couldn't miss them. Railway bridges. Traffic roundabouts. Poor sod! A life of crime and he goes down for the one he never did!' Mum giggled as if this was hilarious.

'Not exactly,' I say. 'It was, "Gary Davis is a grass."'

'Gary Davis the lemon grass,' she said. 'I wouldn't know anything about that. Sounds like your father's department, that. Poor geezer probably gave the police some information about some insane, violent socio-paths like the Krays.'

'Yeah?' I say, meaning, 'Go on.'

'You know, Caryn. The Krays. Gangsters. Big time. Famous for looking after their own. And severed heads in the fridge. Bodies in rolls of carpet. Pet cats in the chip pan. Made the East End what it is today. I expect he put one of

them inside and the dear old loving East End has never for-
given him. Here's to Gary Davis, the lemon grass. Good for
him!' She raised her glass. There was a piece of prawn shell on
her chin.

'Lemon grass,' she murmured. She was talking to
herself. Not to me.

9

BLIND MIND MORNING

Saturday morning, I'm in the usual rush. Dress. Eat. Run Mango. Get to work. I switch on the telly for the time, tip Rice Krispies into a bowl and fish round in the drier for a clean pair of pants. Last night with Craig spools through my head.

We didn't do anything special – just mucked about, but we had such a brilliant time. When I rushed out of the shop on the dot of six thirty, there he was, waiting for me. I hadn't even checked my face in the mirror. It was Saturday, we were meant to be going out.

We raced back to mine and took Mango to the park in the last of the light. Craig threw sticks and Mango did her vertical lift off and snatched them out of the air. Then Craig climbed into one of the empty niches on the war memorial and stood to attention, with one of Mango's sticks pressed against his shoulder like a rifle. I tried to make him laugh, but he stood as still as a real statue while I made faces at him and even when I flicked Mango's lead in his face, but when I nipped his leg just above the knee cap he gave a roar and collapsed out of the niche on to the ground. I ran, and Craig chased me through the trees and Mango went mad when he caught me and kissed me. He told me he'd wanted to see me!

He knew I was going out, but he wanted to see me first. He didn't want to wait till tomorrow. I was thinking, he likes me! He really does like me. I was so happy that when we got to Starburger, I danced to their crap music in front of all . . .

. . . Kobir Chowdhury. The words chop my daydream into bits and chuck it into the bin!

. . . the student who was the victim of a brutal attack in East London last week, tragically died at the London Hospital in the early hours of this morning, without recovering consciousness. A farmer from Devon who buried . . .

I fumble for the switch and zap it.

A tiny sun blazes in the brown teapot on the kitchen table. The freesias that Mum brought home on Thursday are turning to tissue paper. I'll throw them out in a minute when I've finished eating my breakfast. It's so quiet in here I can hear the Rice Krispies snapping and crackling away. It's a sad sound, like the crackle that comes from the telly when you switch it off.

Of course he isn't dead. They've got it wrong. They'd have said if he was dying. And they didn't. They said critical, yes, but no one ever said anything about dying. Someone's made a mistake. They'll announce it soon, then they'll look stupid, saying someone's dead when they're not.

I can see my face in the teapot, twisted and yanked out of shape. A tiny sun shines brightly over my shoulder. I don't want to look at it. I put my finger on it and blot it out.

Shit! Shit! Shit! No! It's not true. He can't be dead. He took a battering, that's all. Lots of people take a battering and they don't die. He's fit. He's young. He plays footie. It would take more than a kicking to see him off. Someone's lying. He's not dead!

I squeeze my eyes tight shut, but I can still see the teapot with the sun in it, sharp and glossy as a postcard. I grasp it with both hands and hold it tight while the heat seeps through my palms. I hold it until I can't bear the pain any longer, then I shove it away to the other side of the table.

No. It's true. Of course it's true. It's what you'd expect of him, after all. You could have hung in there, Kobir, if you'd wanted to. You just didn't want to fight. Any more than you wanted to fight down there on Canal Road. You gave up! You let them do it to you! You're just gutless, Kobir!

I stick my hands under the cold tap until it looks as if I'm wearing scarlet gloves.

Kobir is dead. So? I am sorry and all that . . . of course I am . . . and I wish he hadn't of died . . . of course I do . . . but what can I do? Nothing. If there was anything I could do to bring him back – anything – I'd do it like a shot . . . of course I would . . . but what there is . . . is nothing . . . and that is a fact.

'Hey! Caryn! I'm right with you!' Warwick claps eyes on my face and is over the counter in one hop. 'Dad!' he yells. 'Till!' His hand in the small of my back half guides, half shoves me into the back room and all the time he keeps up a stream of non-stop, meaningless chat.

'Now I know what "white as a sheet" means,' he goes. 'I've honestly never seen anyone look as bad as you do now. You look truly terrible. Sort of whitey-green and shiny. As if you'd glow in the dark. You're not going to throw up, are you?' But he has the kettle on. And he's put a Pot Noodle in the microwave. And he takes off his jacket and puts it round my shoulders before pushing me into the chair. The warmth of his body is still in it. I snuggle down into the quilted lining and let it warm my bones.

He dumps half a packet of sugar into the coffee and hands it to me. 'Get that down you. You ain't eaten I bet?'

I force some coffee down. A bit burbles back and Warwick hands me a bundle of tissues. 'Take your time,' he says, 'but get it inside you. You need the sugar.' When I've swallowed half a cup of coffee, he unwraps a Twix, pulls out one of the fingers and breaks it in half. 'Now food,' he says. 'Eat. No arguments. Anything else you want, I'll get it, OK. You only have to say.'

It's taking me time to get used to this new caring Warwick. I thought he'd do one when I finally showed my face at the shop forty-five minutes late. 'What's got into you?' I croak. 'You joined the St John's Ambulance?'

Warwick grins. 'That's more like it. What do they put in them Twix bars, ay? Nah, June knows all about first aid. If you're a boxer, they're always doing it on you and you get to know about it. And he's passed some of it on to me.'

One Pot Noodle, two Twix bars and two cups of coffee-flavoured sugar later, I'm beginning to unwind, but Warwick's features are gelling into his 'this is serious' face. He has perched himself on top of a stack of Persil cartons and is worrying at a pile of newspapers that are lying next to him, slipping and sliding them over each other. The noise is getting on my nerves.

'Caryn,' he says. 'Caryn, are you ready for this?' He

bundles the papers up and tosses them on to the floor. They land with a thud and fan out in the tiny space – and there, all over the floor, all over my feet, is Kobir's face. Every single tabloid and broadsheet carries the picture of Kobir's poor battered face on the front page.

I pull my feet up on to the chair and squat above the sea of newsprint. The headlines scream up at me in letters two inches high:

MY SON, MY SON
A NATION'S SHAME
RACIST CRIME CAPITAL
HE NEVER STOOD A CHANCE
COMA BOY DIES
KOBIR STRUGGLE OVER
ASIAN BOY DIES AFTER ALLEGED
   RACIST ATTACK

Without moving my feet, I reach down and flip over the pages. They've dug up untold pictures of Kobir. The usual family stuff. The fat baby. The little kid with his football. A day out at the sea. A pokers-up-the-bum wedding group. A shop portrait. His life his family his friends, who wanted to remember him growing up – because they were proud of him. Because they loved him.

They were gutting.

All this time I'd never, ever, even once, thought about Kobir the person – what he was like. And here he is in a stupid photo-shop pose, staring straight at me over the book he is pretending to write in. Floppy quiff, peachfuzz moustache, he's got no style, but he looks nice. He's trying to look serious for the picture, but you can see it is an effort. He can't take the sparkle out of his eyes. He's a guy who looks easy with himself – someone who had a life and knew where it was going.

Before they booted his brains loose.

I feel choked and I don't want Warwick to see my face, so I squint down at the papers on the floor again. At first the print is blurred and then it comes into focus.

My eyes take in a bit here and a bit there – an attack of unprecedented savagery, brutal and brutish, fiends in human shape, an escalation of racially motivated attacks.

Then it jumps out at me, from where it's hiding at the bottom of the page – MURDER HUNT – Police are launching a murder inquiry into the death of Kobir Chowdhury, the student who was beaten to death in East London last week. Inspector Dave 'Stinger' Nettles said . . .

Murder! I must have said it aloud cos Warwick's head is nodding.

'That's right!' he says. 'It's gotta be murder! You must've known that.'

Did I? Maybe I did! Probably I knew as soon as I heard it on the telly. Just the word scared the shit out of me! MUR-DER. A hot shudder jolted through my back, like someone had injected boiling water into my spine.

'Warwick,' I say. 'This isn't happening to me, is it? Tell me it isn't happening.'

'Too right!' snaps Warwick. 'It isn't happening to you! What happened, happened to him!' Then he says, 'I'm sorry, Caryn. I didn't mean it like that. That wasn't fair. You must be feeling terrible.'

Terrible? Try panicked. Try paranoid. Try petrified.

Murder does not belong in real people's lives. Murder is serial killers, sex maniacs and Satanists. Mad axemen, gangsters and robbers. Twisted, evil, ruthless perverts. Pathetic, no-hope, saddo losers.

Not real people. Not me!

'It's not fair!' I wail. 'I didn't ask for this to happen! It's not my fault! I was just there, that's all.'

One of the boxes Warwick is sitting on has a split in it. A trickle of soap powder on the floor is becoming a pool – white flecked with blue. The smell fills the hot little room, sickly sweet with a synthetic prickle that catches in my nose and makes me want to sneeze.

'Caryn, take it easy, I say. Think a little. This is serious stuff now. You gotta stop reacting and start thinking. You understand what I'm saying to you?'

'What are you saying to me, Warwick?' I ask.

'What are you going to do now? Go to the police? Get in touch with that Inspector Nettles? What?'

I stare at him. I can't believe what I'm hearing! The police?

'Think about it, Caryn. These guys are dangerous. They've done this before. They are probably gonna do it again! Someone else is gonna get hurt. Or killed.'

'Warwick!' I say. 'Would you go to the police?'

'Me?' He points a finger into his chest. 'You are jokin' me, Caryn? A black guy walk into a police station of his own volition?'

'Yeah. Well. I'm not a grass either, Warwick. The police can find those guys on their own. If that's what they want to do! IF!'

'Caryn, what I'm trying to say is that you could be in danger. These guys are not pussycats, you know. They could be on your case right now!'

How'd he figure that one out? OK, so Rosie gave me the once-over in the street, but he's not a mind reader. I didn't have a label with my name and address on it pinned to my jacket. He's got no way of knowing who I am and where I live. And anyway, if I keep my mouth shut, which I fully intend to do, he's not going to bother to find out, is he?

10

gooners

They came out of nowhere, out of the crowd that comes to Miranda Street for stuff it can't find in Tesco – air-gun pellets, bait, knitting wool, model aeroplane kits, koi food. I've looped off my usual route home to stock up on Mango's favourite pink bone-shaped dog biscuits that the pet shop sells from plastic tubs on the pavement. And Miranda Street is a laugh, which is what I need right now. I check out Fantasia Tattoos – I'm getting a yin-yang dolphin on my shoulder, or maybe a bluebird. Then, because the Algerian patisserie is just over the road, I start fancying one of their burnt custard tarts.

MUR-der! The word throbs inside my head. It's been pounding away all day, DUH-duh. DUH-duh. The beat is driving me mad, so I don't see them coming, not till I'm right up against them – a two-headed man-mountain towering above me and blocking my way. I don't step aside. I wouldn't do that, not for arrogant low-life scum who think they own the street. For a second it's a stand-off. I clock a big guy in an Ellesse T-shirt, with a gut that wobbles over his belt, and behind him a dark guy in a leather jacket. I don't have time to take in anything else. The wobbler half-turns and shoulder-barges me off the pavement. It's not an accident. He meant to

do it all right. He turned, took a step back and barged me
with all his weight.

I fly! I mean it. I travel! Over the pavement. Into a
lamp post. On into the road. My feet don't touch the ground.
When they do, my legs fold up under me like Romey's buggy,
and I collapse in a heap in the gutter. Where I stay, while the
street rocks and rolls around me.

By the time I pick myself up, the pain has kicked in.
My shoulder, where I collided with the lamp post, is a ball of
sheer agony.

I stagger over to the patisserie. I'm dabbing up the
crumbs of my second custard tart when I make the connection. The man in the leather jacket, I've seen him before. It
was the man who put the wind up Craig in the pub a week
ago. It was Meatface!

Clouds of sandalwood-scented steam roll out to meet me as I
open the front door. Mum getting glammed up for a big night
out. Voices murmur from the kitchen. Layla is there. I know
why she has come, but I don't want to talk, not now. I need
some space. I want to soak my sore shoulder in a long, hot
bath till Craig comes.

They are in a huddle round Davina's laptop. Mum
is in her dressing gown – mauve bedspread material with a
woolly scarf round her middle – and a towel knotted round
her head. She is staring into the screen like it was a mirror
and she'd just found a spot. One hand is in front of her
mouth. The other lies flat on the table. Two of the nails are
painted midnight blue. A nail-varnish brush, propped up on a
biro, has dripped an iridescent blue pearl on to the paper

underneath it. Layla is by her side, clattering away at the keyboard.

'Stop panicking, Gina!' Layla is saying. 'It's gotta be in here somewhere. It's just a question of finding it . . . Hi, Caryn. You a'right?' Neither of them look up from the screen.

'I'm fine,' I say.

'I can't have lost it!' Mum is moaning to herself. 'It's weeks of work! Nearly my whole project! Davina'll kill me. I couldn't have not saved it! I couldn't, could I?'

'You ready for the party then?' says Layla. 'You'd better be. Mum's been cooking all week.'

Ari's party! Shit! I'd been looking forward to Ari's party all week. I'd got everything I was going to wear planned down to the last sequin and I couldn't wait to show Craig off to everyone. But tonight! How was I supposed to party tonight? After everything that had happened?

'Yeah, later on, maybe,' I say. 'I'm not feeling in the mood right now. I fell over in the street and I don't feel too good.'

Layla's hands fly up from the keyboard. Then she makes a grab for my hand and jerks it downwards. It's my bad arm and I yell, but she doesn't take any notice. 'Well, you'd just better get in the mood, that's all, because you're coming,' she snaps. 'You're expected. Ari will be really hurt if you don't come. You know he will. And Mum will be hurt.'

'Caryn!' Mum has noticed I'm there at last. 'What has got into you? You can't miss Ari's party! You're not ill, are you?'

'She's been in a mood all week,' mutters Layla. 'That's why I came round.'

Layla was right. I couldn't not go. Ari was like my brother. He'd always been there for me. He used to walk us home from school sometimes if Bridget had been held up, and he chased Mickey Crisp all the way to Old Ford Road for doing the drawing pin trick on me. He would be hurt if I didn't show.

'I'll be fine in a bit,' I say. 'Craig and I'll be there.'

'Craig?' goes Mum. Not looking away from the screen.

'He's just someone I know,' I say. 'He works along the road from me.'

'Yeah! Got it!' yells Layla, punching the air above her head with both hands. 'You'd saved it in the wrong folder, Gina. It's with your letters, not in your college work file. I knew it had to be in there somewhere!'

Mum throws an arm round Layla's neck. 'You clever thing. You've saved my life. Stick the kettle on, Caryn. Let's celebrate.'

Under cover of the gushing water, Layla hisses furiously in my ear, 'I knew you'd be like this. I'll never speak to you again if you don't come. Let it go. Live your life. It's got nothing to do with you. It never did have and it doesn't now.'

Craig is half an hour early! I am still getting dressed and Mum is watching *Casualty*. She's an addict. She watches it every Saturday, stretched out on the sofa in her going-out clothes, but she never puts on her make-up until it's over because it always makes her cry buckets. She tries to be polite – 'Hello Craig. How nice to meet you.' – but her eyes keep sliding back to the screen. And I'm desperate to be alone with him, so I forget about my mascara and bundle him out of the house.

As soon as we are in the street, he puts a hand round the back of my head, pulls me towards him and kisses me. He says, 'Are you OK, Caryn? No one thought he was going to die, did they?' Then he says, 'Let's go somewhere we can talk.'

I think – Craig? Talk? – but he's grabbed my hand and he's off down the street, towing me along behind him.

The Volvo is his idea, an old estate dumped on the dead-end road that runs alongside the old Seaman's Cemetery. The trees that overhang the cemetery wall have dropped their sticky stuff all over it, and the outside is rough with dust and grit and bits of twig and leaf. Instead of smooth metal, it feels like sandpaper.

'No,' I say, when Craig unlocks the door. No way am I letting my white trousers anywhere near that! But he runs his hand over the seat, and the upturned palm he shows me is spotless. Inside, there's a fusty, damp-metal smell, but at least it's private. The only noise comes from trees creaking and straining in the wind. A piece of torn off notebook is sellotaped to the windscreen and on it says in faded biro, 'You can go in and snog all night. As for breaking in you will pay.' Craig pulls it off, screws it up and puts it in his pocket.

'Who does it belong to?' I ask.

Craig grins and touches the end of my nose with his finger. 'Ask no questions . . .' he says. 'Just say it belongs to a mate of mine.' He puts his arms round me, squeezing me tight, kissing my face and knotting his fingers into my hair. It's what I've wanted all day, to be alone with Craig, with his arms holding me, but I never realized just how much. Tension tumbles away from me in huge chunks. I don't even try to talk any more. I breathe in his smell as the day blots itself out.

I could have stayed there forever, but Craig pulls away from me and leans back against the car door. The wind is getting up and the trees in the cemetery are rustling and groaning.

'Would you believe them trees?' he says. 'I never knew trees could kick up such a row.' Then he looks up at me through his eyebrows, all serious, and says, 'You sure you're OK, Caryn? I've been worried about you all day.'

'I'm fine now,' I say. I try to snuggle back close to him, but I can't because he's pulled his leg up on to the seat and all I get is a knobbly knee. 'Kinda numb now. I just want to wake up tomorrow and find that none of this happened.'

'So,' he goes. 'Have you decided what you are going to do?'

Decide? Do? Just the words make my brain go into melt-down. 'I just don't know, Craig. I keep trying to think about it, but nothing seems right. Warwick says I should go to the police, but I don't know.'

'The police! You off your head, Caryn? You think the police are going to shift their backsides for a dead Paki? And if you grass, nobody round here will ever speak to you again ever. And that includes me. You know that, don't you? Your life won't be worth living.'

Do I know it? I know it all right. He doesn't have to tell me. But then . . . I flap my hands in frustration. 'It's murder now, Craig. And I am the only witness. Aren't I supposed to do something?'

Craig gets his leg back down on the floor and pulls me

back close to him. With the tips of his fingers, he strokes the inside of my arm, letting the nails just catch on the soft skin. It sends hot shivers right through me.

'You've been watching too many police serials on telly, Caryn. This is real life. Murder's no big deal. Not these days. Not round here. There's murders every week in the *Gazette*. The bottom line is he's dead, and you can't do anything for him. I mean, if there was something you could do, yeah, I'd be right with you, but there's nothing. So. End of story!'

Murder no big deal? It was my turn to pull away. I just stared at Craig, trying to read his face. What was he on about? I'd seen those vermin hurl themselves with everything they'd got into that dark bundle on the ground. They weren't holding anything back. It was a big deal for them! And Kobir? And Kobir? Wasn't it enough of a big deal for him?

'So what are you saying to me?' I squeak. My throat is so tight I can hardly get my voice out. 'Kobir is dead. They battered him till his brain bled. What are you saying, no big deal?'

'Caryn! Caryn! Calm down!' Craig taps out the rhythm on my leg. 'You're getting all emotional. Think about it. I mean, what is murder? A guy wants to kill someone, he thinks about it, then he goes ahead and does it – that's murder. Premeditated, right? If it's not premeditated it's not murder, it's something else. Manslaughter. Accidental death. I dunno. But not murder. Now, what you've got to ask yourself is those guys who were giving the kid a kicking did they mean to kill him, or were they just trying to teach him a lesson? What do you think, Caryn? You were there. Did they mean to kill him?'

Did they mean to? How am I supposed to know? I'm not a mindreader. What I do know is I've never heard so many words come out of Craig's mouth in one go. Where are they all coming from?

Craig doesn't wait for me. 'They never meant to kill him. It was an accident. These things happen.' He put his arms round me and squeezed me tight. 'No point in making a song and dance about it, is there?'

I sit there without speaking, listening to the trees carrying on overhead. The dashboard is thick with dust. I make whirly shapes on it with my finger, but the dust has been there so long it is part of the plastic and my finger doesn't leave a mark. I'm tired. Everything is going blurry. I can't hang on to all the thoughts that are swirling around inside my head any more. Murder? Or not? Who cares? Perhaps Craig is right and it is time to let it go? I grab hold of that one idea and pull it round me like a comfortable old coat.

'Caryn. Caryn. Don't you think?' Craig's voice drones in my ear from a long way off.

'Yeah. Probably. You're right. We're late. We gotta go . . .' We'd missed Bridget's dinner. I wrench open the door of the Volvo and set off into the dark to the party.

11

MOOD FUN FLIRT

The party is banging! The sound hits us as soon as we turn into the street. Bums are squashed up against open windows and bodies spill out on to the steps! In the middle of the road, a girl in a red mini skirt is laying into her boyfriend – he's holding her off by her wrists while she thrashes about, trying to land a kick on his legs. The crowd on the steps laugh and jeer – all except one guy who is lying full length on the garden wall. His eyes are closed and he looks as peaceful as if he was sleeping in his bed.

We shove our way in and the sound almost bounces us right back out again. It's so thick and springy, it's like walking into a mattress! I want to rip it out by the handful and stuff it into my ears until all the spaces in my head are crammed to bursting. Voices clatter and slap against each other; shouts, bellows, shrieks of laughter and giggles jet up above the background roar. An energy charge surges through me from my heels to the top of my head. It's brilliant. I grab Craig's hand and we're in.

A drink first – a Pils for me and a Coke for Craig. I get one down my neck and take a couple of others for later. The kitchen is packed with weird uni-types, from everywhere in the world, it looks like! Two tarty sorts in tiny skirts and with what looks like clingfilm round their tits, are swigging vodka from a bottle. Under the clingfilm their nipples look like pennies. Old guys with grey hair lean against the worktop shouting and waving their arms about. Two little kids of about eleven, a boy and a girl, dressed in black, with loads of gothy eye make-up, are melting Mars Bars in a pan on the hob. They make a grab for the Clingfilms' vodka, slop some in on top and turn up the heat. A guy in a silver leather jacket, with about a hundred rings and studs in his head, is propped up in the doorway. His hair is sculpted into silver waves and he stands as still as a statue as we shove past him towards the sound.

The living room is blue. Twists of blue paper shade the lamps and blue fairy lights loop and spiral round the walls. Blue and white disco lights pulse to the beat, and catch the pearly blue smoke that hangs over the stomping, heaving bodies. The sound is dark and wild. The fat base-line plucks at my guts and locks on to my bones. It sucks me in. I pull Craig in with me and I dance. I dance to hammer my brain. To empty my head. To blank out everything but the music. I thrust and whirl and stamp until today is a tiny disappearing point at the end of a long tunnel. Craig is right with me, flinging himself around until he has cleared a space for himself the size of a sofa!

My can seems to have emptied itself and I go back into the kitchen for supplies.

Craig hooks his fingers into my waistband. 'I'm hanging on to you,' he says. 'I'm not letting you outa my sight in this madhouse.'

But in the kitchen he bumps into someone he knows

from the gym and while his back is turned I help myself to the Clingfilms' vodka too. They are too glazed to notice so I take a swig and then another and another. Then I grab a couple of cans and set off back to the blue room for a birthday dance with Ari. Craig rushes after me. All these uni-types make him nervous.

I dance and dance – with Ari. Ari and his girlfriend Alizia. Alizia and Craig. Craig and Layla. People keep packing in until there's no room to move. They keep bumping into me. One girl barges me right in my sore shoulder and knocks me off balance – so for the second time today I lose control of my legs. This time I'm not standing for it. I shove her back so that she stumbles into the wall and yell at her to get outa my face – and then her boyfriend's there saying, 'What's going on?' and Craig has grabbed hold of the boyfriend's shirt-front with one hand and he's shoving him against the wall. His other hand is pulled back in a fist.

Hey! Hey! Craig! Caryn! Take it easy! It wasn't her fault! Stay cool! You fell against her! Caryn fell against her! It wasn't her fault! She didn't do anything! Ari and Alizia and Layla are all crowded around me, all talking at once. I need to find some space. Some air. I push my way up through the crowds on the stairs. Upstairs is green – green shades and green fairy lights. Two guys are drumming, weaving Latiny rhythms in and out of the beat that pounds up through the house. Naked to the waist, their torsos are covered in body paint: jungly shapes and dark outlines that could be any colour in the green light. All around them, bodies lie, chilling, listening. One girl is dancing by herself in the middle of the room. Arms high in the air, she shuffles and sways to the music, in her own world. She is wearing a sarong and a bikini top and she is painted all over too. Then she turns and I can see that on the back of the bikini she's only fixed a pair of wings! Gauzy golden wings that wobble about as she moves!

'Caryn! Why did you run off like that? I lost you.' Craig flops down on the floor beside me.

'It's cool,' I say, and lean against him because the floor is tipping to one side. I hold up one hand in front of my face and swim it backwards and forwards, wiggling the fingers. It looks so funny I hold up the other one too. My seaweedy green hands make me laugh so much I hold them up in front of Craig's face but he doesn't think they're funny. Craig's face, when he sees the wings, cracks me up.

'Weird or what?' I say.

He hisses in my ear, 'Now I know what my nan meant when she talked about a flighty piece,' and I just get the giggles and I can't stop. He's saying, 'I dunno, Caryn, I thought students were meant to be clever,' but then he says, 'Come on, Caryn, let's get you outa here. You need some air.'

Getting out is hard. The floor won't stay still. It keeps coming up to meet my feet – just like the ferry when Dad and I went Christmas shopping in Calais. The stairs are worse – they've got steeper and some of the steps are a long way down. I keep tripping up and crashing into more people. Craig goes down in front of me, making a path through the crowd. Then he disappears and the next thing I know, I'm sitting on a chair in the garden and he is walking towards me carrying a bottle of water.

The garden is pure magic. It's jam-packed with people and the music hangs over it like a sort of net holding everybody in and the rest of the world out. Night-lights and candles in bottles and jars line the walls and a little stubby tree is hung with more lights. The moon is up, huge and silver, and I can see the light on top of Canary Wharf Tower winking at the sky. Two gardens away, a bus turns into the bus station. The headlights come straight at us and it looks as if it is going to drive right into the garden, but then it turns away in the other direction. A siren sounds in the distance. A plane lifts into the sky from City Airport. The whole city thrums around me. Its energy runs through my veins and I am part of it. I'm not just me any more – I'm part of the huge city that breathes in and out with me. It's a brilliant feeling. I fling my head back and spread my arms wide.

'Can't you feel it?' I say.

'Feel what?' says Craig.

'The city. Breathing all around us. Can't you feel it? It's alive!'

What does Craig do? He takes the top off the bottle and tips water all over my head! Not a great gush, but a thin stream that runs over my hair and pours down my face. I duck out of the way and run off down the garden, but he chases me in and out of all the people – and when he catches me, he presses himself up against me, pinning me against the wall.

'You're mad, you are,' he says, tipping the whole bottle over my head. 'Look at the state of you. You trying to embarrass yourself, or what?'

I shake my head and spray flies off my hair. I push it back off my face and squeeze some of the water out. It hasn't washed away my mood. I really want Craig to feel it. I want him to be part of the breathing city too. I lean back against the brick wall and point up into the sky.

'Where d'you think that plane is going?' I say. 'Paris, New York, Hong Kong?'

'City only do Europe,' he says. 'So it's not New York or Hong Kong.'

'Wouldn't you like to be on a plane right now?' I say. 'Going somewhere the other side of the world. Like Bali. I saw a programme about Bali on television. It was amazing! Wouldn't you love to go to Bali?'

'Nah,' says Craig. 'What'd you want to go there for? It'd be too hot. You wouldn't know the lingo and even if you did you'd never know what was going on in their heads. They could be talking about you and you'd never know. And you'd have to eat tofu!'

'Craig!' I have to laugh. He is hopeless. He'll never understand about Bali. How everything was just perfect. Better than I could even dream: white sands, palm trees, sky and sea a dream turquoise blue, and a little girl in a red dress, with a golden head-dress like a crown.

Craig puts his arms round me and pulls me close to him. 'So you'd go off to Bali and leave me, would you? I'd miss you if you went away.'

'Would you really?' I say.

'Course I would!' Craig's face is pale and I can see the moon in his eyes. 'I really like you, Caryn. I don't say that to everyone, but it's true. I like you a lot. I want to keep on going out with you and I want you to go out with just me. Not anyone else, just me. Will you do that, Caryn?'

Why did he have to say it now? When my hair is a

soaking wet mess? When it is sticking up in peaks round my face? When I remember this moment, I'll move it back in time to when we were first sitting in the Volvo, when I'd just fixed my hair and my make-up was still on my face!

'All right,' I say. 'If that's what you want.' As if I have to think about it. As if I am only doing it because he wants. Not because I want. And I do! I do!

Then he puts his arms round me and kisses me and he's never kissed me like that before. And I've never kissed him like that before. At first it's just the skin of our lips touching and it's like little needles pricking me all over. Then his mouth opens and my mouth opens and I don't know which is Craig's mouth and which is mine. My bones melt like chocolate and if he wasn't holding me I would slide down the wall into a heap on the ground.

After a long time, I pull away. 'Let's go!' I say. 'Let's go back to mine.'

Back at my house, you wouldn't think it was the same Craig. It's like this evening never happened. He is tense and twitchy like he was the first time we went out. He stands in the middle of the room looking big and gangly as if he's afraid of taking up too much space. Then he flops down on the settee and stays there for about a second before he bounces back up again, and prowls round the room fiddling with things. He flips through my mags, checks out Mum's CDs and then examines her collection of blue glass medicine bottles, picking up every single one of them, weighing them in his hand and turning them upside down to read the writing underneath. He even just about ignores Mango, who is flirting with him like mad.

He says, 'A'right, girl?' and ruffles her round the ears, but that is all.

I grab his hand and try to pull him down next to me on the settee. He keeps hold of my hand but he won't sit down. I put my other hand on top of his. He does the same. It's like that stupid game we used to play in primary school. I lean my head against his arm and then he does sit down beside me and puts his arm round me, but his arm is draped round my shoulders like a scarf. It's not pulling me closer to him.

'What is it?' I say. 'What's the matter?'

'Nothin',' he says. 'There ain't nothin' the matter.'

I kiss him and he kisses me back and soon it is getting like it was in the garden. Then my top has come off and my bra is coming off and Mum might walk through the door any minute now. You never can tell with her.

I grab my clothes. 'Let's go upstairs,' I say.

I shouldn't have said it. He leaps to his feet. 'What about your mum?'

'She won't be back for ages,' I say. 'She'll have gone to a club somewhere. And if she does come back she won't care. I can do what I like.'

'No!' he says. 'I can't. Not tonight. There's things I gotta do tomorrow morning.'

'What things?' I say.

'I've got early training. We booked the gym for eight. My mates'll kill me if I don't show.'

He gives me a quick hug, then he pushes me away from him. 'It's the truth,' he says. And he just about runs out of the door.

Mango jumps up on to the settee beside me. I put my

arms round her and press my forehead into the hard bone of her skull. What is it with Craig? I can't make him out. One minute he's all over me and the next he doesn't want to know. And it's been like that from the start.

I feel terrible. I thought he really liked me. I thought he meant those things he said in the garden. Then why did he walk away from me when we were gettin' it on? Was it because *I* came on to *him*? Does he think I'm some kind of slag now? Is it as stupid as that? But I don't think it is. Craig shot out of the door like something was chasing him. What is he so scared of? Is it me? Mum?

'He's full of secrets,' I whisper in Mango's ear. 'And I'm going to find out what they are.'

12

DEVIL

I must have been asleep for all of ten minutes when Mango barks right in my earhole. I snap awake struggling to sit up, my heart thumping and all my senses stretching into the darkness around me.

'Hey, Mango,' I say. 'What is it, girl? What's up?'

She ignores me, leaps off the bed and skids over to the door, whining anxiously.

I lean out of bed and fling an arm round her neck. 'It's OK, girl. It was a bad dream.'

She's not having it. Her hackles are up. She knows it's not OK. She can feel my heart pounding right through the duvet.

She wrenches herself free. It's light enough for me to see her, ears pricked, head cocked to one side, listening at the door. Every now and then she barks a shrill, angry bark. There's someone in the house! Where? In the living room? Mum's room? Outside my door? All the doors and windows are locked and bolted, but someone broke into Liselle Winch's house through the roof, and dropped down through the trapdoor on to the landing.

I stare at the door. I'm paralysed by fear and I can't move a muscle. The duvet is pulled up to my chin. I feel like

I'm made of duvet. All of me, arms, legs and head, stuffed full of useless feathers!

All at once Mango shuts up. She walks round in a circle twice, wags her tail at me then plonks her backside down.

'Have they gone, girl?' I croak. She looks at me out of the corner of her eye and shoves her nose up against the crack under the door.

After about a hundred years, I open the door a chink, but I don't get a chance to listen because Mango thrutches through it and hurls herself down the stairs. Her racket echoes in the tiny hallway – a rolling growl that erupts into harsh, aggressive barks. It's a wild animal sound, scary enough to see off anyone who is still in the house. I creep down after her, one step at a time, leaning on the wall to steady my trembling legs, my bare feet silent on the stairs.

There's nobody there. No scuffling footsteps or slamming doors. No draughts of cold air from open windows. But something is not right. I can sense it – and my skin puckers between my shoulder blades. I grope for the light switch, but before I find it, the smell hits me – a strong, earthy, outside smell. Somewhere inside me, I know what it is and, just as the message gets through to my brain, I stumble into it. Like wet string on the soles of my feet. Lumpy and cold and sharp with stones. Ripped out by the roots and stuffed through the letterbox.

Grass!

He's found me.

Rosie has found me.

I grab the keys from the hook and struggle with the

deadlocks, but when I get the door open the street is deserted. Mango is nearly choking herself trying to break free from my grip and give chase. Then, out of the corner of my eye, I catch a flicker of movement in the distance. A tiny black dot is coming towards me across the Fields. A black dot I could pick out of any crowd of a million or so. Mum!

I kick Mango out of the door and slam it shut, shovel the rooty mess into a binbag, whizz away the mud and give the skirting a wipe round with a tea towel. When Mum lurches in through the door the kettle is coming to a boil and I am stretched out on the settee trying to look half asleep.

'Hi, Mum.' I fake a loud yawn. I'm still breathless from all that rushing around. 'You got Mang? I had to let her out for a wee and when she saw you coming she shot off to meet you.'

Mum's a bit wobbly on her feet. There are black rings of smudged mascara round her eyes. It takes her a while to answer and I watch different expressions trying to get a hold on her face. 'She's here. You can go back to bed now. D'you want me to bring you a cup of tea?'

'No, ta. I just want my bed. D'you have a good night?'

'Not bad. We all ended up at the Blue Note. They had a samba band from Brazil.' Mum giggles. 'It must have been a good night, I can smell summer in here. Summer Sundays in the garden.' When she says summer, she makes inverted commas with her fingers. And does a little twirl.

Back in my room, I wrap my duvet round my shoulders, pull my chair over to the window and light a ciggie. Outside, it is almost light, but it is a cold blue world. No colour. No contrast. Just blue. Nothing is moving. Not a thing. I could be the only living thing on the whole planet. I inhale deeply and rock myself backwards and forwards until my chair creaks.

So. Rosie has found me.

He only clapped eyes on me once, through the window of the white transit – and somehow, he's tracked me down.

I walked away from the transit, just another kid on the street. He'd given me a scare and that was the end of it: that's what I'd told myself. For a start, the chances of seeing him again were a million to one. You can go years without seeing people who live on the same street round here. And even if he did bump into me, yes, he'd had a good look at my face, but if I was wearing different clothes, he probably wouldn't even recognize me.

How wrong can you be?

Those mad, screw-head eyes had bored right into my head, read me, knew me. He saw where I worked, who my boyfriend was, where I went dancing, what I ate for breakfast. I couldn't have any secrets from him: he knows me inside out. And if I even think about telling, which I won't, he will know.

And the grass through my letterbox is a warning. Don't mess with me, it's saying. Keep your mouth shut. Don't try anything. You can't hide. There's no escape from me. Whatever you do, wherever you go, I will find you, because I know you now.

My arms are covered in gooseflesh. Every single hair is standing to attention. I try to stroke them down flat, but they're not having it. They bounce right back up again. Don't try and fool us, they're saying. You're scared shitless. We know!

The trees in the Fields are black blots on the blue

world. The sky is lightening up, but the trees are still holding on to the night in their branches. They are the deepest sooty black right out to their twiggy edges and I can't take my eyes off them. I feel like I am being pulled in . . . into the blackness . . . and then, as I stare, I get the weirdest idea. I know where the night goes. The trees suck in the night, through the twiggy fuzz at the end of their branches, into their hearts and then into the night caves deep among their roots. And I am falling, tumbling, whirling, head over heels down into the dark . . .

I must have been asleep because I come to with a jolt. It's light now, a clean, washed sort of light. A silver Central Line train is crossing the viaduct the other side of the Fields. I can hear cars on the main road. Not the normal background traffic drone, but cars, one at a time. I've never heard that before. Lights are on in some of the flats. They could switch them off now, if they wanted. Down the road from me, someone comes out of a house and sets off over the Fields. I watch him till he has got right over to the other side. There are quite a lot of people about now. I push myself out of my chair and fall forward on to my bed.

13
just landed

I was woken up by the phone – again. It was Dad this time, ringing from the No-name Cafe Bar. The electrician had only just turned up to work and the chippie couldn't lay the new floor until the electrician had finished and the new custom-made bar top didn't fit and the decorator was due in tomorrow, so Dad had to get down there and sort it but Jill's morning sickness was atrocious so he'd had to bring Romey with him, but the bar was a death trap for babies, so could I come and take the lad off his hands? Just for a couple of hours? Please?

'Dad,' I groan. 'I never slept a wink last night and I've got a splitting headache.'

'No problemo!' says Dad. 'The espresso machine is up and running and the fresh air in the park will do you good.'

I stick my head under the shower and drink a carton of orange juice, which takes care of the headache, but then I have to deal with yesterday. Yesterday is coming back to me in flashes. Not all at once. Not in the right order. All muddled up like a set of holiday snaps that fifty people have flipped through already. Gauzy golden wings. Raw grass smell. Bobbing, dancing faces. Kobir's picture. Water, trickling past my eyes. A thread of soap powder.

I crawl back under the duvet and pull the pillow over my head. It won't hurt Dad to hang on to Romey for a bit longer. Yesterday did my head in. Yesterday I came on to Craig. Yesterday Kobir died. I squeeze my eyes tight shut, but the pictures still scroll through my head. I'm going to have to get up and do something. Make a bacon sandwich. Run Mango. Swim thirty lengths. Kill myself. Then the phone rings again. It is Craig.

'I'm in the Fields,' he says. 'I'm on your bench. Look out of the window and you'll see me.'

I pull my blind up and there he is. Standing on my bench, waving both arms above his head. I drag on a tracksuit and run out of the house. I don't even bother to put on shoes. I jump up beside him and he grabs my hands and waves my arms in the air too.

'Don't get the wrong idea about last night,' he says. 'You were off your face, and I had training.'

He is wearing sweats too. I run my fingers down his arm, and feel hard muscles are under the soft stuff.

'I wish you had stayed,' I say. 'Someone only shoved a load of grass through our letterbox in the night. I was by myself.'

Craig frowns. 'What, he's found where you live now? You must be shitting yourself?'

'Not really,' I say, and it's true. The night – that was one thing, but in the morning sunshine, with Craig's arms round me, what could Rosie do to me? It would take more than a bit of grass to scare me now!

Craig pushes me away and holds me at arms' length. 'Just watch yourself. And keep your mouth shut. Cos if you don't, he's going to come after you, and if he does, it won't be very nice, cos he's not a very nice person. Know what I mean, Caryn?'

It makes me laugh, Craig trying to be the man. He hasn't even seen Rosie but he has to pretend he knows. It makes me go all warm inside and I don't want him to go away.

'Come and have some breakfast,' I say. 'Come to the park. I've got to take Romey – Jill's sick.'

He doesn't even think about it. 'Do me a favour,' he says. 'I get enough of babies at home. You go. Take your mate. Have a nice time.' He jumps down from the bench, and jogs off across the Fields.

So I phone Layla and tell her to meet me. I have a lot to tell her . . .

Dad wasn't lying. No-name Cafe Bar is manic! The electrician has half the floorboards up and he's whacking the joists with a hammer and chisel. What's left of the floor is covered in stuff – tools, coils of wire, stacks of wood, so there's nowhere to put your feet. The stairs down to the basement toilets are not in place, and if you walked over the edge of the hole where they should be, you'd break both your legs. The chippie is sanding the bar top. The row does my head in and the air is solid with dust. Dad and Uncle Al are in the back yard with Romey, who is struggling to get out of Dad's arms and into the plaster that has leaked out of the bags stacked against the wall.

Dad thrusts Romey into my arms. 'You're a diamond, Caryn! His stuff's all packed up in the buggy. Jill put some bread in for the ducks. Just get him out of here before he kills himself. Here, take this for ice creams and things.' He shoves a note into my top pocket. 'Give me a couple of hours then I'll fix us a late lunch. Bring Layla.'

Mango hates it in the bar. Her ears are right back, and she is pressing herself against my leg, trembling with every burst of noise. I strap Romey in the buggy and get them both outside. Then I brush the dust off his cheeks, out of his hair and away from his clothes and we settle down to play 'Whoops Tommy' on the pavement while we wait for Layla.

Outside, the cafe bar is looking good. It's an old baker's shop and Jill's designer mate has hung on to the old shop front and painted it orange and blue. A lot of people are going by on their way to the park or the Sunday market, and when Romey gets bored with 'Whoops Tommy' I start teaching him new words: 'lay-dee', 'dog-gee', 'bay-bee'.

We don't have to wait long for Layla. She rushes up, gives Romey a kiss, pokes her head round the door of the bar and says, 'Wow! What a madhouse! Let's get outa here! D'you want dog or baby?' It isn't a question. Layla always takes Romey on the grounds that I can have him any time. And, while she's always polite to Mango, she doesn't go a bundle on dogs.

Layla is teaching Romey different makes of cars. An East End lad needs to know his wheels, she says, so while we're still on Commodore Street, she's keeping a lookout for the right makes. I'm bursting to talk about last night.

'Hey! What about the party?' I start.

'I bet you're glad I made you come now,' says Layla.

'You had a good time, so don't lie and say you didn't. And the light ropes – weren't they excellent? I did them!'

'And the types there! The man with the silver hair! What was he like? Where does Ari find them?'

'You know Ari. He just gets on with everyone. He collects people, like I collect CDs. Only he's not fussy, like I am. Hey, guess what, right! I met this great guy! He's a friend of Yanni's. He's a trainee in a bank in the city and he's twenty and he's so cool. Wait there! Look Romey, Romey, a Golf GTi. Say it, Romey – Golf. Golf.'

'You seeing him again? Is he phoning you? What does he look like?'

'He's going to ring me next week and we're going out Saturday . . . What about you and Craig then? He was all over you last night. He's really into you, isn't he? Hey, Romey, a Beemer 325 SEi. You can say Bee-ma, Romey. Bee-ma.'

'What do you think of Craig then?' I know you should never ask and I never meant to. It just sort of popped out.

Layla missed a beat. No one else would have noticed, but I did. 'He's all right. Quite nice looking. Not my type, but all right.' She gives the pushchair a little shove and catches it before it rolls away. Then she says, 'He doesn't say a lot, does he?'

So? What does she mean, he doesn't say a lot? He doesn't have to talk all the time. Not everyone has to gab on like a maniac all the time.

'And he's a bit quick with his fists,' says Layla. 'He really went for Liam. He was going to smash his face in and he would have done if Yanni and Ari hadn't stopped him. And for what?'

She makes me mad sometimes. She thinks she can say anything she wants. She always thinks she knows. When Craig went for Liam he was looking out for me. But I wouldn't expect her to see that – because Craig doesn't work in a bank and drive a posh car she thinks he's rubbish.

'I'm only saying what I think. If you didn't want to hear it, you shouldn't have asked.' Layla pushes the chair away from her and catches it just as it goes out of reach.

Romey loves it and squeals his word, 'Mo!'

She pushes him a bit harder, waves and calls, 'Bye-bye, Romey.' Then we turn the corner into the pedestrian precinct, and she pushes him right away from her. He sails through the Sunday shoppers, shrieking with laughter. Layla chases after him, laughing too, her black hair streaming out behind her. People turn and smile as they go past.

Let them go, I think. Let her go with her stupid stuck-up ideas. Who does she think she is?

Suddenly, I can't see them any more. We are getting near the market end of the precinct and the crowd swallows them up. I'm not bothered. Layla can get lost for all I care – and I know they are only just ahead of me, somewhere in the crowd.

Then – I just get this feeling. The danger spot in my back has come alive. The sensitive spot that prickles when something is wrong. Something, or someone behind me means trouble. What kind of trouble I don't know, but it's definitely bad news.

Who is it? I turn round – almost! Then I pull myself back. Think, Caryn! *If* there is someone there! *If* I know they are there, but they don't know that I know, I am one step ahead. Right? So I carry on walking, weaving in and out of the shoppers, acting like I've lost someone and I'm looking for them somewhere in front of me. Which is what I am doing, but I just make it more so.

I see Layla and Romey almost immediately, but I don't want them to see me. Not yet. The bit of the precinct we are in is wide and lined on both sides with market stalls, making an alley between the shops and the stalls. I duck in-between kiddie's dresses and hair ornaments and scuttle along close to the shops, keeping Mango on a short leash. When I'm certain that I'm a long way past them, I come out into the middle of the precinct and look back the way I've come. I really go for it. I shade my eyes with my hand and stride about calling, 'Layla, Romey'. I see Layla almost immediately, but I pretend I don't so that I can get a really good look at everybody who is behind me.

Nothing unusual. Nothing suspicious. Not a thing. Everything Sunday normal. Mums. Dads. Kids. Bulging shopping bags.

Layla rushes up to me. 'Caryn! You didn't have to run off because of what I said. You know what I'm like. I thought he was all right. I did.'

'I thought there was a baker's shop round here,' I lie. 'I wanted to get some bread for the ducks.'

I should feel relieved, but I don't. The sensitive spot is still there. And the feeling that something is going on won't go away . . .

14
rugid

The duck beach is a pongy mess of churned-up mud, duckshit and feathers. Romey loves it and as soon as he sees it he goes mad, pointing and shouting and trying to climb out of his buggy. Loads of other people have decided to bring the kids to chuck bread at ducks, and they're all hanging out, chatting and grabbing at the little ones before they fall in the water. The sads are there too. The pigeon man who makes himself as still as a tree and lets the pigeons perch all along his arms and even on his head. The old ladies with carrier bags full of crusts who've given every single duck its own name.

'Poor old things,' says Layla as she undoes Romey's straps. 'Promise me you'll never, ever let me get like that. I never want to be that old and that sad.'

Romey hasn't quite got the hang of feeding birds. He holds on to the bread and won't let it go. The ducks ignore him, and he squawks in frustration, so we go and sit on the little rail on the edge of the path and spread the bread out on the ground – and then we can't see our feet for ducks. Romey is so excited he can't even squeal. He bats at the air with his hands, then bends down and tries to gather up the ducks in his arms.

It's all normal Sunday morning stuff. Mums and dads

and kids having a nice time in the park. So why can't I relax? Why is the danger spot in my back still there? Why is it still telling me that something is wrong?

Mango is sitting quietly beside me – too quietly for a dog surrounded by a hundred birds. As soon as she senses that I'm thinking about something else she gives a violent twist to her neck and jerks her head backwards in an attempt to slip her leash. This time I'm too quick for her and I drag her over to a seat the other side of the path, out of temptation's way.

That's when I spot him! On the grass by the willow trees, where the crowd is beginning to thin out. Alone, trying to look as if he's out for a walk, phoning a mate, waiting for the pubs to open. But I don't think so. He doesn't belong here. Everything about him is wrong. The black combat jacket. The black baseball cap crammed right down over his eyes. He doesn't fit, and he knows it. His shoulders are hunched into a question mark and he is rocking himself backwards and forwards on the balls of his feet while he peers into the crowd.

I'm back with Layla in half a second flat. 'Get Romey into the buggy,' I hiss. 'We're going to the swings.'

It must be something about the way I say it – for once, she doesn't argue. Romey does though. He hollers and struggles until every single person round the pond knows we are leaving. Between us we manage to get him strapped into his buggy and we set off across the park. We don't say much. Romey carries on yelling until his face turns purple. It's shaming. People are staring and wondering which one of us clobbered him.

He perks up as soon as he sees the playground. He

adores the swings and the baby slide even more than he loves the duck pond. While I unstrap him I have a good look round. There's no sign of Black Hat. He hasn't followed us. Everything looks normal. No sign of anything suspicious. Everything's fine, I tell myself. I'm jumpy after last night, letting my imagination run away with me. I let Mango off the leash and settle Romey in a baby swing and Layla and I take turns to push him.

'Well?' goes Layla. 'What happened back there? Romey was having a great time.'

'There was someone from school I didn't want to see,' I lie. 'Larraine Parks. I hate her guts.'

Romey is in baby heaven. His eyes are as round as burger buns and his mouth is a big 'O'. I push him higher, then a bit higher, and all the time I'm chatting away to him, 'Romey, up you go. Romey, up in the air,' and watching his eyes so I'll see if it gets too much for him.

Which is why, when it finally happens, I am not ready for it.

Romey flies away from me, through the air. A dark bulk appears behind the swing – a green and black bulk that sets alarm bells in my head frantically jangling. Meatface and Wobbler, who barged me in the street yesterday, are standing behind the swing. Romey is flying towards them, crowing with delight. I launch myself after the swing with all my strength. Too late. Meatface has leaned forward and grabbed the swing. Then he lifts the swing high above the ground. As high as he can reach.

'Romey!' I scream and when I scream Romey screams. Layla screams. Mango barks.

Meatface holds the swing high in the air, and my little brother dangles against the restraining bar.

'Let him go!' I yell. I run at him, grab his arm and hang on, but I can't pull his arm down. So I hit hit hit him with my fists, and Layla hit hit hits him, but it's like hitting concrete. I kick him. I try to kick him in the balls, but he can twist himself out of my way without letting go of the swing. Nothing I do makes any difference. None at all. I'm crying and yelling, 'Let him go! He's a baby! He hasn't done anything! Let him go!'

Then Wobbler grabs me and twists my arm behind my back, so I have to stand on the tips of my toes. 'I wouldn't do that if I were you,' he says.

I can hear Romey's shrill, terrified screams. 'What do you want?' I say. 'Just tell me what you want!'

Wobbler spins me round and yanks me towards him. 'Listen to me,' he hisses in my ear. 'You saw something you shouldn't have done. Something that was none of your business. Now you just keep your nobby little nose out. If you open your mouth, it won't be you we come after, it'll be him! And he won't be a pretty baby any more!'

Wobbler shoves me away and I stumble down on to the ground. Meatface lets the swing go. Gives it a little flick and Romey plummets down. Layla makes a flying leap forward and catches him. I pull Romey out of the swing and hold him close. Over his shoulder I watch Wobbler and Meatface stroll away through the trees.

The whole playground comes to life. People crowd round us.

'Are you all right?'

'Is the baby all right?'

'Sit yourself down.'

'What was all that about?'

Then a woman produces a mobile. 'I'm phoning the police,' she says.

The police! No way! Not now! 'Run!' I shout at Layla. 'Just do as I say. Run!' Still holding Romey tight I race across the park. Layla races after me with the chair. Mango bounds along beside us, barking excitedly at this new game.

We run through the streets until we get to May's caff. May takes the overspill from Callegari's and people go there when they feel like some peace and quiet. I need to calm Romey down – his eyes look like bruises against the milky white of his face, and every now and then he lets out a thin, stuttering wail. I rummage round in his tool kit, find his bottle and shove it in his mouth.

Layla is getting cappuccinos and chips. She plonks the tray down on the table and lifts Romey off my lap. 'I'll take him,' she says. 'Look at your hands. You're shaking like a leaf. He's never going to shut up while you're like that.'

May clucks around, worried about the baby.

'He fell off a swing in the park,' I lie, but then it's almost true. I can see Romey's little body falling through the air. I can even hear the smack as his head hits the ground. It plays over and over again in my head like a memory. Like it really happened.

Romey shuts up as soon as he gets the bottle in his gob. Layla leans across the table and jabs my arm, hard, the fingers of her free hand squeezed into a point. I can see white round the edges of her nostrils. She's fuming.

'Right,' she says. 'I wanna know what's going on. You've been acting funny all morning. Since the shops you didn't listen to a word I said. And why did we have to run at the duck pond? Were them two lowlifes there? And who were they? You've seen them before. I know you have. I'm not blind, you know. What have you been playing at? Romey could've been badly hurt back there!'

I tell her. I tell her how Wobbler and Meatface shoved me into the traffic in Miranda Street on Saturday – but then I thought they were just normal, arrogant, mean, low-life scum. I didn't connect. Then I tell her about the grass through the letterbox.

Layla's eyes snap wide open. 'So you reckon in the park, that was them, right, the guys from the white transit? Car-ryyn! I never for one single minute thought that they'd come after you again. I thought they'd just wanted to scare you in Martineau Street, you know, for a bit of fun, but then I thought they'd leave you alone. I mean, I . . .' She reaches over the table and grabs my hand. 'Hey, Carry, you all right? No wonder you were shaking.'

Layla hasn't called me Carry since we were kids. 'They did leave me alone,' I say. 'Nothing happened last week. Then Kobir died. That made everything different. It's murder now. He died yesterday morning. I was at June's all day and they've been on my case ever since I walked out the door.' My voice is flat and matter-of-fact, but that is not how I feel. A huge question is putting itself together in my head. A question I can't speak because just thinking about it makes the back of my throat go wobbly.

'How did they find your house?' Layla is working it out. 'They followed you – right?'

'Yeah. Something like that. But Lay!' It came out in a rush. 'How did they know where I was this morning? The only people who knew I was going to the park with Romey were you, Dad and Craig. And Uncle Al. Dad only phoned this morning. How did they know where to find me?'

'And my mum,' says Layla. 'She knew.'

Romey has drained his bottle and is falling asleep in Layla's arms. His eyelashes flutter and a little shudder shakes his body. I want to reach out and stroke his downy skin. I want to gather him in my arms and breathe in his smell but I can't. I can hardly bear to look at him. I keep seeing his face as he falls through the air. All because of me.

Layla is fiddling around with her cappuccino, pressing the back of the spoon down into the foam and watching the spoon shaped hole fill up with bubbles again. Neither of us have touched our chips.

'You know what this means?' she says. 'They must be watching you. Watching your house. Watching June's. Watching school. Following you in the street. They must have you under constant surveillance. They must have spies everywhere.'

Spies. Yes. The guy at the duck pond. I knew I was being followed. I felt the watching eyes on my back. He must have followed me from my house to the bar, through the markets, into the park – and called up Wobbler and Meat-face from the duck pond. And they must have been watching from the trees . . . waiting . . .

I feel weird. Like I'm made of glass, as transparent as an empty coffee jar. One more blow and I will shatter into smithereens.

I take a look round the caff. Which one is it? Who is watching me now? The stubbly old geezer in the corner? The woman with the bike lock and panniers full of vegetables? The man marking the *Racing Post* with pink highlighter? It could be any one of them.

'Hey, Carry. Listen, right.' Layla's hand is on my shoulder. 'You gotta do something now. They're going to come after you again. That big brute holding Romey up in the air, he was getting off on it. I could see it in his face. The more terrified you were, the more he liked it. He's going to want to do it again, Carry. You can't do this on your own. Tell your dad. And your Uncle Al. Let them sort it.'

I just stare at her. Where is she coming from?

'Didn't you hear him?' I say. 'If I open my mouth once, they'll go for Romey. And the next time they'll really hurt him! I can't tell Dad. I can't tell anyone. And that goes for you too, Layla.'

15

HAARDS

'Nah man! What's goin' on? Where is everybody?'

Kendra and I are standing at the school gates. I rang her last night and asked her to meet me at the sweet shop near my house. She never asked why, so I never told her that I'm paranoid just walking down the road. On the way there I was checking my reflection in shop windows to make sure I wasn't being followed. Looking right and left and over my shoulder when I crossed the road. Watching the ground for shadows creeping up behind me. Constant surveillance: that's what Layla said. And that means every single minute of the day.

On a normal Monday the playground is packed. Twenty games of footie all going on at once. First years racing round like lunatics, everyone else gossiping about the weekend. The game. The party. The club. Who got a snog. Who got dumped. Who got into a fight. Who got trashed. Today, it's a wide empty space. Half the kids have stayed home. There's just one game of footie, and anyone can join in. Mostly the boys play and the girls go straight into the building.

There are almost as many teachers as kids out there. Walking up and down in twos and threes, trying to look normal. Teachers *never*, ever come into the playground if they're not on duty. That's what I say to Kendra.

'Yeah! And just look at 'em!' says Kendra. 'Look at Doherty and Mr Singh. Cuddling up so close you'd think they slept together last night. They're shitting themselves.'

Barnowl and Keith are standing between the gates and the main entrance, where they can see the whole of the playground. They are facing away from each other and their heads turn slowly as they scan every inch and every corner. Barnowl is head of maths, and when there is trouble, he sorts it. Keith, the caretaker, is always right in there with him. He's right next to Barnowl now, the man in black, twirling the bunch of keys that hang on a long silver chain from his belt.

Twenty or thirty boys are not playing football. They are gathered on the steps up to the main entrance. Jason and Gary Cook and their mates – some who you don't see in school a lot. Some of them I haven't seen since year nine. They don't even look like they belong here any more. Their faces are hard and clenched. Not kids' faces. You can already see where the lines are going to go when they are old. Even the teachers keep out of their way.

We're almost at the main entrance when Kendra grabs my sleeve. 'Wait there!' she says. 'They're up to something. They wouldn't be here if they weren't.'

Fong is just in front of us. Fong is tiny even for Vietnamese. You could get three Fong's into some of these guys. She weaves a path through them as quickly as she can without looking, as if she's hurrying. She knows not to look scared. She knows to keep her eyes down. Then Jason Cook takes a step sideways – right into her path.

She has to stop dead. She skips to one side. Jason does the same and they are face to face again. Their shoes touch.

Fong ducks out of his way – first one way, then the other, then back again. Her long black hair sways as she moves. She is too quick for Jason, but this time Gary Cook slides in front of her. So close she has to jump back and she stumbles down a step. Gary laughs. Fong tries to skip round Gary, but Darren Boyd and Aidan Coughlin move in to block her way. They are a wall in front of her. She looks up and meets their eyes.

'What's up love, don't you want to go into school today?'

'What's your problem, slit-eyes?'

Fong tries to shout, 'I tell my brothers about you! They come for you with machetes!' But her voice is thin and shrill and they all laugh.

Then Liselle Winch walks up the steps. No one moves. Not one of them. Not an inch.

'Did you see that?' says Kendra.

'Yeah, cos she's white!' I say.

I carry on walking until I'm nearly at the bottom of the steps then I walk up them. They don't take any notice of me. They don't even see me. But then I step sideways so Aidan Coughlin is right close up in front of me. He is a big guy and he is on the step above me. My nose is between his tits. He could zip my head up in his jacket if he wanted. His chin has a sort of nick in it – like they didn't finish joining it up properly. But I don't have time to think about that. This voice comes out of me. 'Get out of my way!' it says. 'I want to come past.' I hurl the words at him like stones.

I'll never know what would have happened next because Kendra knocks into me running, grabs my arm and hauls me past Aidan Coughlin and into the building. She won't let me stop until we get to the girls' toilets, then we collapse laughing on one of the benches.

'You was puttin' your life on the line back there, wasn't you? What were you thinking of? You OK?' goes Kendra.

'Nah, man,' I say. 'I'm cool. What about you? They let you through then?'

Kendra throws back her head and laughs – her mouth is so wide open I can see her back teeth. 'They never stop me. They're too busy workin' it out – is she black or is she white? Doh! And while that is going through whatever they got instead of brains, I'm in there, grab you and we're out the other side.'

You'd think once would be enough, but I only do it again! In tutorial this time.

Doherty decides that we have to say something about Kobir's death, and not just let it go by.

'I feel that it is extremely important for every single one of us to acknowledge the feelings that we have about this tragic event. I want to hear from every one of you, even if you just say one word, starting with you, Motisir Rahman.'

'Oh, mi-iii-ss.' Motisir sinks his head on to his arms and groans, 'Can't we just get on with the lesson? I mean, we all feel the same. We all think it was terrible. What do we have to say it for? What's the point?'

Doherty puts on her most solemn face. 'I think you will probably find that not everyone in this room feels the same. After all, we have students here from thirteen different countries, thirteen different communities, and, let us face it, it touches some of us more closely than others. And while I hope you're right, Motisir, and we all do think it is terrible, it is important that we are each able to express this in our own individual ways. And if there are unspoken antagonisms between us, it is imperative that these come out.'

Lies, lies, lies, all round the room. It's awful.

He was sixteen, same age as me, right, and he lost his life, that's not right, no way is that right . . .

Whoever done this, they should pay, innit, miss? They should pay good . . .

My brother knows his cousin, miss. He never hurt nobody. He didn't deserve to die . . .

What about his family, miss, I feel sorry for his family, especially his mum, just think how she feels . . .

Yeah, and his dad, they aren't ever going to get him back . . .

I feel sorry for his brothers and his sisters, them families are close, aren't they? I'd be gutted if anything happened to my brother . . .

Yeah, and I feel sorry for his aunty and his cousins . . .

That's when it gets bad. A voice from the back sniggers, 'An' his cat – his cat must be missing him. I feel sorry for his little pussy cat, miss.'

Another voice sneers, 'And his budgie, miss, I'm sad about . . .'

It's horrible! They don't care! They're dissing Kobir. Dissing his family. His friends. It makes me so mad! And words leap out of my mouth again.

'It's made me think, miss. It's made me think about what it's like to be afraid to walk along the street on your own, to have to take abuse all the time, and not to feel safe ever, even in your own home.'

Then someone starts at the back of the room, 'Paki-lover! Paki-lover!' They make it into a noise like spitting.

I turn round. 'Who said that?' I shout. Whoever it was I want to . . . I can see it, in front of my eyes, like a film . . . *I grab Larraine by the hair and I smash her head into the wall. I keep doing it until the wall is red. Then I swing her head round and I can't see her face for red!* . . .

'All right, Caryn. That's enough. Thank you. Thank . . . you.' Doherty is frantically patting the air with her hands.

Kendra grabs my arm for the second time. 'Caryn! What's got into you today? You on something? Just take it easy, OK!'

I definitely do not want to risk anything like that happening again – and you can't trust teachers not to stir things. Teachers never know when to leave things alone.

There's a landing at the top of the fire stairs above the level four classrooms which only the caretakers use. Teachers never go up there. Why would they, for a locked door saying HAZCHEM? Me and Kendra hide ourselves up there at breaktime with a load of munchies from the machine, enough to last till lunchtime, and a girl called Shona from Business Administration follows us up there. Shona is whinging on and on about a party Kendra went to Saturday night.

'Didn't he ask about me? Didn't he ask where I was?'

'Nah,' goes Kendra. 'He never said nothin', right?'

'Did he say anything about me? He must have said something about me?'

'No!' snaps Kendra. 'He never said anything about you. He never even mentioned your name. Not once. All right?'

'OK! Keep your hair on!' goes Shona. 'I only asked. You don't have to shout. What's your problem anyway?'

'My problem?' says Kendra. 'My problem is that I'm missing art. I'm doing Hokusai's wave in found materials, and I want to be in the art room getting on with it not sitting on my backside up here because a stupid little git should have thought before he went down Canal Road by himself.'

A stupid little git? I go cold. All over. Kobir died because he was stupid? That wasn't it. Kobir died because someone else wanted him dead. Not for any other reason . . . 'Kendra!' I say. 'He can walk wherever he wants. He can walk down Canal –'

A bag of Hula-Hoops smacks into the side of my head.

'Lighten up, will you, Caryn!' says Kendra. 'It's a joke, all right. A *joke*.'

A joke! 'Well it wasn't very funny, was it? Was it? Kobir is dead. Dead! Or are you forgetting?' I am shouting at the top of my voice.

Shona's mouth is hanging open.

At least Kendra looks embarrassed. She rolls her sweater over her hands and drags it down over her tummy. 'Yeah. Right. I'm sorry. I'm hacked off – that's all. I've been looking forward to this morning. I got all my stuff together, I done my drawings and I want to get on.'

'Who's stopping you? Am I stopping you? Go away and do your stupid wave or whatever if that's what you want.' I can't let it go. I'm so angry I want to hit her.

'That's what I mean. I have to feel right. I have to be chillin' – not all churned up inside. Anything I do now would be crap. And it's all your fault. Carrying on like that. What's got into you? You're not usually like this.'

I ought to tell Kendra what's going on. We're mates, after all. It's not fair not to. I open my mouth to speak – but before the words can come out, Natalie's voice pops into my head and I see Nat down by the canal, in front of my eyes. Her face is all pink and she is waving her arms about and shouting at Kendra, 'You were dissing Kobir and his family. You didn't go for them at all. You went for the buzz!'

'You seen Natalie?' I say.

'Nat? You jokin' me, aren't you? She won't be in today. Or to . . .'

She never gets to finish. 'Wait there!' she says. 'Listen. Something is . . .'

Her words sink into the silence that has crept up the stairwell. Something is going on. Doors slam. Running feet clatter in corridors. Noises you'd never hear over the row of eight hundred kids letting off steam. The background break-time roar is not there.

Then an urgent voice stabs into empty space and echoes round the building – 'Fight! Fight!' But we are already leaping down the stairs three at a time.

'Come on!' shouts Kendra. 'We're missing it!'

The action is in the park just over the road from the school gates. Most of the school is watching from inside the gates, or hanging off the wire fencing, but plenty are in the park too. Two year nines have perched themselves on top of a concrete litter bin. We shove them off and scramble up ourselves.

About thirty boys face each other over an invisible line, ringed by a tight coil of spectators. Everyone you would expect to see is there, and some you would not. Right in the middle are Abdul Mukith, Mujibur Rahman, Iqubal Hussain and Jolil Uddin, faces blank, shoulders hunched deep into their leather jackets. Opposite them, Jason and Gary Cook, Darren Boyd and Aidan Coughlin. Jason Cook is screaming at Mujibur, his face all sharp edges and angles like cracks in a pane of glass. Jason's arm slashes the air.

Kendra does the words – at the top of her voice. 'You shouldn't've said that, you stinkin' Paki. You're dead!'

Mujibur thrusts his whole body towards Jason. Abdul, Iqubal and Jolil close in behind him.

'Come on then! You want some? Come and get it then!' goes Kendra again.

Gary Cook gives a yell, lunges forward and shoves Abdul so hard he staggers backwards. Mujibur hits Jason Cook. Girls scream. The line of spectators pulls back, like a wave going out on the beach. Darren Boyd and Iqubal are on the ground. Gary Cook is giving Abdul a battering. Aidan shoves Jolil – Jolil shoves back. Aidan shoves again – not hard. A lot of shoving is going on.

Kendra, teetering on tiptoe on the rim of the rubbish bin, yells at the top of her voice, 'What's up Aidan? Scared you'll rip your best jacket?' and gets a laugh.

Other kids, arms waving, eyes popping, rush up to the line, scream abuse – then veer off at the last moment and race back to their mates.

Barnowl streaks across the playground like Linford Christie off the blocks. Keith is right behind him. Then someone shouts, 'Knife!'

Everybody screams. I scream. Kendra screams and grabs hold of me. We cling together on our concrete bin.

Everyone's screaming and yelling. Then Keith gets an armlock on Jason Cook and marches him into the building. Jason's struggling and shouting, 'I'll get him. I'll kill the bastard.'

Teachers stream out of the gates.

Then they swoop! Twenty or so, from each of the side streets that run along the side of the school. Armed with baseball bats, billiard cues, golf clubs, they pitch straight in.

Kendra and I can see everything from our litter bin. It looks like some sort of mad game – a jostling, writhing scrum. But it's not a game. Cues jab and thrust. Bats and clubs whirl and smack. Going for the Asian boys. No laughs now. Just grunts and yells and roars that erupt from the concentrated quiet. Nobody is pretending now.

Mujibur Rahman is there in the middle, so are Abdul and Iqbal. Aidan Coughlin and Darren Boyd are fighting with them. Jolil and a lot of others try to run, but they are shoved back into the middle by a ring of billiard cues. They can't escape. They are held there in the middle by the cues.

Barnowl and Keith hurl themselves into the fight. Teachers grab the younger kids and fling them back through the school gates.

Then the next thing I know is I'm flying through the air. The billiard cue hooks through my legs and flicks me off the edge of the bin – like you'd flick a crumb off a clean top. My legs are all tangled up with the cue so I can't get my balance and I go down head first. The ground rushes up to meet me. At the last minute I get one leg down to break my fall – but I still end up flat on the ground with the tarmac an inch from my face. I stare at it for what seems like ages. When I do try to move, I can't for the tangled forest of legs around me. Jumping over me. Knocking into me as if I was a bag of rubbish.

Then Kendra gets to me. 'Outa the way. Go on. Move! Let her up!' and pulls me to my feet.

Then the sirens come and it is all over. The park empties. Except for Mujibur Rahman and Gary Cook who stay locked together oblivious of everything around them.

16

Her Brisk

'Look at yourself! What a mess!'

Kendra is right. Soaking wet jeans, muck all down my front and a grazed hand.

'What d'you want to go and do that for?'

We're still standing by the rubbish bin. As soon as the sirens sounded, there was a mad scramble for the school gates. Kids piled through and launched themselves back into playing footie, just like they'd never been gone. Jason Cook's mates didn't care – and they wanted everyone to know it. They sauntered off towards the main road, looking hard. The guys who came with billiard cues all raced away in different directions. The police car screamed right up to the main entrance of the school. Kendra and I stay where we are and let it all happen around us. No one cares about us.

'I lost my balance. One minute I was on the bin and the next I was on the ground.' I'm lying again. It's getting to be a habit.

'Well, you could have let go of me,' grumbles Kendra. 'I only went right into the bin, didn't I?' A Colonel Sanders box has fitted itself round Kendra's foot like an extra shoe. She peels the soggy cardboard off with the tips of her fingernails. It leaves a sticky-looking mess behind. 'Yuck! Yuck! YUCK!'

'You scraped your leg,' I say. 'It's bleeding down the back.'

'You seen your face?' asks Kendra.

My face? My face is OK. I ended up flat on my belly and I stared at crunkled black tarmac for long enough, but my face never hit the ground. Did it? I reach up and touch my cheek. I know which cheek to touch. Then I look at my fingers. They are bright see-through red.

'How bad is it?' I say. I think I'm going to be sick.

'You'll live,' says Kendra. 'But you ain't going to look like Kate Moss for a bit.'

You can forget school this afternoon! No way am I going into school looking like this. I must look like one of the bag ladies who sleep outside Whitechapel Station.

'Come on,' I say to Kendra. 'We're going to Natalie's.'

Natalie lives just the other side of the park on Mast-maker Road. Their flat has got a steel reinforced door and an iron security gate and Carol, her mum, doesn't work. She stays at home all day doing things in the flat.

My face throbs as I walk. I can taste blood on my lips and feel the swelling with my tongue. Now I know about it, my cheek feels like thousands of needles are sticking into it. Natalie squeals when she sees it, shoves me into the bathroom and shouts for her mum.

I cover my eyes with my hands, then I peep into the mirror through my fingers. When I force myself to take my hands away, I see two faces, the one that I see in the mirror every morning, and another that looks as if it fell into a tub of Ben and Jerry's Cherry Garcia. I've skinned one cheek, an eyebrow and a blob at the end of my nose. My lip is fattening up. Voices outside are saying, 'hospital' ... 'stitches' ... 'tetanus jab', and Carol is shoving me down on to the side of the bath and swabbing my face with Dettol. It stings like she is using it neat, but I don't shout.

'Will I have a scar?' I ask. I can just about live with a sore face – but I'll be gutted if they've scarred me.

'No-ooh!' she says. 'It's only a graze. It looks worse than it is. Here, give us those filthy clothes. I'll stick them in the washing machine for you. They'll be done in a tick.'

Natalie and Kendra are in the living room, and when I am all wrapped up in Nat's dad's dressing gown, I go in there too. Kendra left her shoes in the hall and she's sitting there in her socks. Carol brings tea in on a tray and sits down next to Nat on the settee.

'Looks like I missed all the fun,' says Natalie. 'What happened?'

Kendra tells them. I tune out. Nat's mum has changed the room again since last time I was here. She changes it all the time. One big question is going round and round inside my head. Did they come to get me? Was getting me at school today the next thing on Rosie's list? Or was it just a fight?

The room looks just like a picture in a magazine. Leather settee with matching armchairs. Knitted cushions, which button up like cardies. A huge picture of Natalie and Carol, with hair blowing across their faces. Not one speck of clutter or mess anywhere. Even the remote is tidied away in its own pocket.

There had to be a fight. No way Mujibur and his gang

were just going to let Kobir's death go. Teachers knew. Kids knew. Jason and Gary Cook knew. They put the word out and their mates came along. That's what happened. It was nothing to do with me. I was just in the wrong place at the wrong time. Again.

Natalie and her mum crack me up. They look like twins sitting next to each other on the settee. They've got the same straight blonde hair, only Nat's is longer, the same pink and white skin, and today they're even wearing identical sand and blue Nike outfits. You have to look really close to see that under all the make-up, there are lines at the corners of Carol's eyes.

Why would they bother to come after me again? After yesterday. I'm not going to forget yesterday in a hurry, am I? How could I forget Romey's terrified face? But then again, maybe Layla is right. Maybe Rosie and his mates get off on pushing me around. Scaring me. Hurting me. Like they get off on hurting other people. That's what they are like.

Kendra is laying it on with a trowel – like there were hundreds that streamed into the park with machetes and knives. Then she has to go and say she saw a gun. She is such a liar! Natalie and her mum each grab hold of a cushion and clutch it to their bellies.

When Kendra has finally wound down Natalie says, 'But what were you two doing there? Why are you always in the middle of it when there's trouble?'

Carol puts an arm round Nat's shoulders. 'I told Natalie I wasn't having her going to school today.' She reaches across and rakes Natalie's fringe back with long red nails. 'And I was right, wasn't I, babe?'

'Mu-um!' Natalie shunts herself to the other end of the sofa. 'I go to school if I want.'

'My mum'd have kittens if I said I wasn't going to school,' I say.

'Well, that may be all right for you, dear, but it's not all right for my Natalie,' goes Carol.

'Mu-um!' shouts Nat. 'Just leave it out, will you. I can look after myself, you know. I do know how to keep out of trouble – not like some people round here.'

A mad whoosh of anger jets through me. Shoots the words straight out of my mouth. 'Keep out of trouble! You know all about that, don't you? That's all you ever do! First sign of trouble and where are you? In here behind your security gate. Well someone's got to be out there, you know. Someone's got to know what's going on. Someone's got to . . .'

I run out of steam. Natalie and Carol stare at me with their mouths open. Then Natalie says, 'I don't have a clue what you are on about, Caryn. And I don't see how turning out to watch Mujibur Rahman scrapping with the Cook brothers is *doing* something.'

Carol says, 'And looking at the state of you, I think my Natalie was well out of it.'

Natalie snaps, 'Just shut up, Mum. It's got nothing to do with you!' Then she starts on me. 'I don't know where you are coming from, Caryn. I don't know what is going on round here, but ever since Thingy got killed everyone is picking on me. Well I never knew him. I don't know anyone who knows him. He's nothing to do with me. So I don't understand why you're having a go. If anything happened to one of my mates, I'd be out there for them, and you know it! But not for someone I've never set eyes on in my life and who is not even one of us!'

Natalie is right. And I want to tell her. But the words aren't there any more. There's nothing in my brain but empty space.

I should go home, now. I should get out of there as fast as I can, but I can't because my clothes are in the drier. Carol stalks off into the kitchen and I hear her banging the ironing board into place and laying into the ironing. I just hope it's not my stuff she's doing. Natalie zaps on the telly and we all stare straight ahead of us at the screen without saying a word. I don't want to catch Natalie's eye and she doesn't want to catch mine. I'm like, if I don't move perhaps I'm not really here.

We keep this up through spring make-up trends, Crufts champion mutts and a trainee taxi-driver doing the know-ledge.

I feel terrible. What I said to Natalie wasn't fair. How is she supposed to know what has been going on? I haven't told her.

He comes on during the news, which none of us would normally watch, but nobody turns him off because nobody is going to make a move – Inspector Nettles appealing for information about Kobir's murder.

'We don't want to watch this!' I say. 'Turn it off!'

Natalie gives me a look. I can feel it, even though I don't turn to look at her.

'No,' she says. 'This is what you want, isn't it? To be involved in what's going on outside. Well, let's get involved then.'

'Funny-looking geezer,' says Kendra. 'His head's too big. Looks like someone added an extra inch just above his ears!'

He doesn't like being on telly. Maybe he thinks everyone will be looking at his head because he lets it sink into his chest and he mumbles the words of his prepared statement one at a time, as if they don't make proper sense to him '. . . appeal to the public . . . vicious, but I regret to say, not unprecedented attack . . . increasing at an alarming rate . . . apprehend the perpetrators of this heinous, and I use the word advisedly, this hateful crime . . . were you in the vicinity of the attack . . . did you see Kobir?'

Then he seems to change gear. He leans forward. He lifts his face out of his chest and looks me straight in the eye. 'Did you see Kobir on his way home from school? Did you see his friend? Did you see anything unusual near Canal Road on Friday twenty-third of September? Someone did. I know you are out there! What about you, mums and girlfriends and wives? Have you washed any bloodstained clothes? Because someone has blood on his clothes. I know you suspect something. So, I will ask you again. Come forward and tell me what you saw. Come forward and tell me what you know. I intend to catch these scum – for that is what they are, scum. And I will catch them. But I will catch them quicker if you help me.'

'Dream on!' says Kendra. 'We don't grass round here!'

'Right then,' says Natalie. 'We've seen it. You happy now, Caryn?'

17

MEAN ASIA

I'm officially off school. And I'm bored. I've had a lie-in, taken Mango to the park, and now I'm supposed to be chilling, but I can't settle. *The Matrix* is on the video, but I haven't a clue what it is about. I want to know what happened after the fight. Was anyone else hurt? Who were the gang with the cues? Why had they come? Everyone will be talking about it and I'm stuck here missing it. I can't even phone till dinner time.

I was flat out on the settee yesterday watching telly when Mum came in and plonked a load of shopping down on the table. I was so starving I leaped to my feet to see if she'd bought any yoghurts or Hobnobs or anything else I could eat and, for a second, I forgot about my face.

She gave a shriek. 'My God! Caryn! What happened to your face?' Then she grabbed hold of my head in both hands and dragged me over to the light to inspect the damage. I told her that there was a fight at school and I got knocked over. My voice was slurry because I was speaking without moving my lips. It hurt to talk.

Mum's like, 'Has anyone looked at that? Has it been properly cleaned up? Do you think we ought to go to Casualty? Shouldn't it be covered up? You don't want any germs getting in.' Her eyebrows were up near her hair, which meant that she was really stressing, and she was pulling things out of the kitchen drawer and throwing them on the work top. 'We must have some Savlon somewhere. I know I bought some for emergencies.'

I told her that Carol had cleaned it up and put a bucket of Dettol on it and that calmed her down. Carol used to be a nurse. Then she gave a long sigh and said, 'I don't know, Caryn! I suppose this is all to do with that poor boy who died. It's bound to bring out all the tensions in the community. Sometimes I wonder if it will ever end. Perhaps you'd better stay off school for a couple of days. Let things settle down a bit.'

Did I hear that right? A day off school? Mum? How stressed is she? But I wasn't arguing. School was the last place I wanted to be now. 'You sit down, Mum,' I mumbled. 'I'll put the kettle on and then we'll put the shopping away.'

In the end I go to work early. It's a horrible day. The wind blows grit in my eyes and picks up the rubbish that has collected by the bins. A paper cup chases me all the way across the Fields. The trees by the opposite fence have sprouted fruit the size of watermelons – but when I get closer I can see that they are only plastic carrier bags filled with wind, which have blown up there from the supermarket car park over the road.

There's a crowd round the till. I check them out through the window before I go in. Warwick and Ezra, Ez's girlfriend, Simone, and Simone's friend, Marcia, are all in a huddle over something Simone has got in her hand. I lean on one of the trestles outside the shop and twist to one side till I can see what it is. More pictures. Warwick must have collected another batch from the processors. They must be good too – Simone and Marcia wouldn't usually bother with pictures that aren't of themselves.

My plan is to slide past them into the back of the shop and get stuck into whatever needs doing. I don't want Simone to see my face. You wouldn't find her anywhere near trouble. She cabs it everywhere just so she doesn't have to risk her outfits in the street. And I definitely don't want Warwick to see it before he has to. He'll only fuss.

Fat chance. I have forgotten that trouble is like oxygen to Simone and Marcia. Simone must have breathed me in because I swear she starts speaking while she still has her back to me. 'Hey, Caryn! Had a fight with your boyfriend?'

Then it's Ez's turn. 'Hey, Babe! You had an argument with a truck?'

What can you do? 'I walked into a lamp post,' I say. 'After I fell downstairs and before I shut my head in a door.'

All Warwick says is, 'Hey, Caryn, come over here. Get a look at this.' As I turn round, I can see his face tighten up and he doesn't say anything.

Simone hands them to me. Prints. Glossy, black and white. Last Wednesday's vigil for Kobir. The whole story. My guts go into slow spin. I flick through the pictures because they are Warwick's, but I hate doing it. I want to fling them away through the open doorway. I want the wind to pick them up and whirl them away from me with the rest of the yesterday's rubbish it's chucking about the place.

First, solemn faces in the crowd. Asian, white and

black, in close up, smudged by the candlelight that fuzzes into the dusk like ink on wet paper.

Next, an Asian woman stands above the crowd on a makeshift platform. Three young guys, arms folded across their chests, faces like masks, make a solid wall behind her. An old man with a white beard and a long white shirt stands beside her. In one hand she holds a mike away from her face, as if she is afraid that it will spit at her. Her other hand wrings and twists the folds of her sari. 'Kobir's mum,' says Warwick.

Then you can see the mood is changing. Something is going on in the crowd. Can you photograph tension? Warwick can. His lens has searched it out. In the thrust of a head. In the rise of a shoulder. In a clenched fist hidden in a sleeve. No light shows between the packed bodies. Heads turn.

Now the woman has flung an arm in front of her face. Her body twists away. The old man is pulling her back and off the platform. Other guys, Kobir's brothers and uncles, surge forward over the platform into the crowd. 'Stones,' says Warwick. 'Some scum at the back threw a stone at her. At the guy's mother, would you believe!'

A man flies from the platform. His arm stretches straight out in front of him into the centre of the picture. His hand must have touched the camera, nearly. His contorted face is a howl of pain and rage.

Now the crowd is separating, sliced in half by a human wedge driven in from behind. Twenty or so guys in black jackets, with balaclavas or baseball caps hiding their faces, chop and slice their way towards Kobir's uncles and brothers, who have leaped down from the platform. I don't want to look. I know what happens. I heard it all at school, every single detail. I thrust the bundle at Warwick and I make myself say, 'They're great, Warwick. They say it all.'

The pictures make me depressed. Those people who carried candles at the vigil were full of hope. They wanted to give Kobir their strength. Now he is dead. And the people who killed him are not going to stop. They are going to carry on hurting and hitting – and killing. Anyone they don't like. Anyone who gets in their way.

I tune back into Ezra, who hasn't shut up all this time. 'You see how they come in from the back? How they split us up? No way that just happen. Someone think that through. Someone sit down and plan it, man.'

'You get hit on the head as well as rubbing your face in the dirt?' Warwick grabs the pictures from me and shuffles through them. 'I don't need you to tell me they're good. I know that. I showed you these pictures for a reason. Here. Take a good look at these. With both eyes this time.'

What is he on about? I'm looking at pictures of the fight that ended the vigil. I've seen enough fights to last me a lifetime! I don't need to look at any more! There are some old men in this one – old men with white beards getting stuck in. And police. A line of police trying to hold both sides apart. But they are just fight pictures. I'm just about to hand them back to Warwick when I see him! Craig! He's quite small, on the edge of the picture at the back, but it is definitely him.

'It's Craig!' I squeal.

A line of boys hang from the hospital railings to get a better view of the fight. Craig is one of them. He's yelling something – a hand cupped round his wide open mouth.

'It's Craig!' I go again. 'Warwick, you idiot, why didn't you just tell me . . .' I never finish what I am going to say. Something else I see in the picture makes my stomach clench up so hard it feels like it's been kicked. There, in front of the railings. Rosie!

Rosie is so close to Craig he could almost touch him. The crowd surges and pulls at itself, but there is a space round him. He stands alone, his face as blank as a satellite dish. He could be waiting for a bus. It makes my blood run cold to see him so close to Craig. I thrust the picture away from me. 'It's great,' I make myself say.

'See! I told ya!' Warwick is staring at me. 'It's the boy-friend, innit? The one who waits for you outside the shop? Who likes energy bars? – Yessir? Twenty Silk Cut? Certainly, sir.'

There is a stack of bleach-free nappies in the store. We don't get a lot of call for them, so they are stacked high up at the back. I drag the ladder into the shop and start packing them into the space between the top shelf and the ceiling. If I scrunch them up tight they'll go in three deep, and all the time I'm squishing and squeezing I'm thinking, Craig lied to me. Shove! That was the night he stood me up. Punch! When he said he had to help Christian out at the pool? Scrunch! And all the time he was at the vigil! But why lie about it? He can go to a vigil if he wants.

It made me feel sick seeing Craig and Rosie in the same picture. Warwick's pictures tell a story. You look at them and start thinking, What are they up to? Who is that? What is she saying to him? And when you've finished looking you feel like you know the answers. But, even though I know Warwick has got it wrong this time, I hate seeing Craig and Rosie in the same story.

Warwick's voice brings me back to now. 'Caryn. Would you come here please?'

Ez and Simone and Marcia have gone, but a couple are taking their time over the chutneys and pickles or he would never have sounded so polite.

'I told you they were dangerous, Caryn,' he hisses. 'Was I right?'

'You were right,' I say. What's the point in lying? Warwick knows the score.

He reaches across the counter and touches my face with his fingertips. 'Don't look too good. Does it still hurt?'

I shake my head. 'Only when I laugh. Or talk. Or eat.'

'You thought about what you gonna do?'

I shake my head again. And then I nod. I hate them. I'm totally paranoid. I know it's not over. Layla is right, they get off on hurting people. They will find me again and what will they do then? And what will they do to Romey? They are evil. Blatantly evil.

'I'm thinking about it,' I say. 'But I don't know what to do. I'm scared!' And I told him how they had found me in the park on Sunday, and what they had done.

'Hnuhh!' Warwick did not sound impressed. 'You don't have to worry about them too much. We know they're evil bastards, but we're not talking Mulder and Scully here, you know. Not by a long way. If they've worked something out, they found an easy way. An' you better believe me on that one.'

18
focus

Craig is avoiding me. He wasn't waiting for me after work last night. I've been ringing him all morning on his mobile, but it's switched off. I rang his home number and spoke to his sister but she said she doesn't have a clue where he gets to. I'm desperate to see him – I haven't seen him since Sunday. I have to know what's going on and why he is lying to me.

Wednesday is his half day, so I race round to Laser to catch him before he leaves. I almost don't get there in time because I'm so nervous I keep losing things – my purse, my keys, my lip gloss. When I do get there, there is a queue of people with carrier bags and clothes folded over their arms and Craig is in the middle of dealing with customers. I slide through to the front of the queue and give the counter a tap with a fifty pence piece.

Craig turns, sees me – and he loses it completely. He can't take his eyes off my face. His customer doesn't seem to notice. She just carries on about baby-rusk on her best jacket. He isn't listening to a word she's saying. He's staring at me. The woman in front of him squawks, 'God knows what goes into this stuff, but it's murder to get out.'

Still without taking his eyes off my face he shouts into the back, 'Mehmet! Take over this lady for me. I gotta take early lunch. I owe you one, right!' And he follows me out of the shop.

He marches off down the road without another word. I have to half run to keep up with him and when I say, 'Craig, where are we going?' he doesn't answer. We are nearly at June's when he turns off into some flats. I know where he's going now. It's where I go to sometimes when I want somewhere quiet to eat my lunch, a square with grass and big old trees and a playground for the kids. It used to be the graveyard once and the gravestones are still stacked along one side, five or six deep. The trees are so old that most of their branches have fallen off and nobody has bothered to cut the grass all summer. It feels wild, like the country – until you see the tags on all the seats. The first one we get to has **Knife Kill Death** scrawled across it in red so we go on to the next. Craig sits down and pulls me down beside him.

'What happened?' he says. 'What happened t'ya face?' He is leaning forward with his elbows on his knees and his shoulders bunched up round his ears, scowling at the kids on the climbing frame who are passing round a spliff. Since leaving Laser, he hasn't looked at me once.

I don't want to make a big deal of it so I just say, 'Kendra and I were messing about. There was a fight outside school and we stood on a litter bin to see what was going on. I fell off and scraped my face on the ground.'

'Did they push you?' His hands are clasped together so tightly that the veins in his arms bulge out.

'Who?' I say. 'Did who push me?'

'Anyone,' he says. 'Did anyone push you? Did anyone try and hurt you? Anyone at all?'

One thing I don't want is Craig thinking that he has to go after the guys who did it, so I make myself laugh and I say, 'No way. Kendra and I were just fooling around. You know. I grabbed her then she grabbed me and the next thing was she was inside the bin and I was on the ground.'

Craig doesn't let up. 'You better not be lying to me, Caryn. I gotta know. Were you pushed?'

I take his hand. I like it when he shows that he cares, but I don't want to have to go on lying all afternoon. 'Leave it out, Craig. I – was – not – pushed. OK?'

At last! That does it. He straightens up, stretches himself and grins at me. 'I had to be sure, right. Come on. I'll buy you a pizza. I'm starving. And it'll go with your face!'

But we don't go for a pizza, not yet. We sit astride the bench for ages, opposite each other, our fingers laced. After a bit we start kissing. The kids on the climbing frame shout and jeer. Craig gives them the finger and they start counting – so we go for it. We get to thirty-eight before they get bored and by then I am glad of an excuse to pull away. The smell of dry-cleaning fluid on his clothes is making my head spin. That and the question I am trying to put into words inside my head. Cool, casual, sort of words – Craig, why did you lie to me about the vigil?

Pizza Esmeralda is the best for miles around and we go there, even though it means a longer walk. Craig is in a good mood now. He holds my hand and swings it as we walk and we chat about what we are going to do with the afternoon. I want to see the new martial arts film. He says fine, but first he has to get his nan's shopping in because he always does on his afternoon off.

I wait till the pizza is in front of us before I say, 'I would have gone to the vigil with you if you'd asked me.'

I should have waited until he had finished eating. He has sunk his teeth into a wedge of Americano with extra cheese and he is tied up in a cat's cradle of cheesy stringy bits. When he does answer it is, 'What vigil?'

'You know. The vigil for Kobir Chowdhury. If you told me you were going, I'd have gone with you.'

Craig looks me straight in the eye, something he doesn't always like doing. 'I don't have a clue what you're on about,' he says.

I look right back at him. His eyes are open very wide and he doesn't blink once. His top lip quivers with the effort of forcing his eyes to stay open and I know he is lying to me. I'd know even if I hadn't seen the photograph.

I have plenty of time. We have king-size pizzas, dough-balls and cokes to get through. 'You know. The vigil outside the London Hospital. A week ago today. For Kobir . . .'

'Oh, right! I'm with you now. You didn't want to go there, Caryn. There was a fight. So I'm told. Christian said.'

'I'd have been all right with you, Craig.'

'No, you wouldn't have been all right with me, Caryn. I wasn't there.'

'You don't have to be embarrassed with me, Craig. I think it's cool that you went. Kendra was there, so was Warwick.'

Craig interrupts me. 'Leave it out, Caryn! Why would I go to a vigil? For some stupid Paki?'

'I know you were there,' I say. 'Warwick took some

pictures. You are in one of the pictures. On the railings outside the hospital.'

That shuts him up. He shoves the last wedge of pizza into his mouth whole to give himself time to think. His eyes slide round, meet mine and slide away again. His eyes are exactly the colour of the mineral water in the plastic bottle on the table. Eventually he says, 'Nah, Caryn. You've got it wrong. It musta'bin someone else in the picture cos I wasn't there. Coulda'bin my cousin. He looks like me.'

His cousin! I want to whack him round the head with the mineral water bottle. How stupid does he think I am? I try to make my voice sound calm but an angry wobble gives me away.

'So where were you, Craig, if you weren't at the vigil? When you said something had come up, what had come up, Craig?'

He snaps back at me, 'I told you, Caryn. Christian rang and said he wanted an extra person by the pool for the under tens' swimming. Ring him if you don't believe me.'

'I thought Christian told you there was a fight,' I say.

'Yeah. Right. Someone told him who was there. Which I wasn't. OK, Caryn? Anyway, I gotta go now. I don't have to listen to this. I gotta get Nan's shopping in. Then I said I'd look after Tyler for my sister. I'll ring you, right.'

And he is gone. Slamming some money down on the counter on his way out. He doesn't look back.

Why is he doing this? Why won't he tell me what is going on? He's supposed to be my boyfriend, isn't he? I'm furious with him. Furious with him for lying. Furious with him for walking out on me. But at the same time a hot squiggle of fear is curling through my guts.

I need some cold water over my head. I need to calm down. I need to think. It is about three o'clock when I get to the pool, via my house to collect my gear, and there is hardly anyone there. The schools have gone and the after-work swimmers won't arrive for hours. Two women are swimming slowly up and down chatting, their heads poked up above the water, and there are a few length swimmers. I dive in and skim along the bottom for a width of the pool, surface, somersault and do twenty lengths of fast crawl. Then I hang on the rail and watch the sunlight bounce over the rippling surface of the water. The swim has cleared my brain – it feels as if it is packed in ice.

When I have got my breath back I do what I always do when I feel stressed. I dive down deep and stay in the quiet pool-world. Headless bodies dangle from the surface, their legs kicking stiffly into the hazy blue water. I push myself further down and the blueness thickens around me. There is no sound at all. Only the column of bubbles flying upward from my lungs connects me to the breathing world. I flip along, moving only enough to stay down. I want the hazy blueness to fill my head so I am part of the water and the water is part of me but my brain won't have it and it starts to click through some of the pictures it has stored away.

Click one – Craig and Mango fight for a stick in the park. Mango's lips are rolled back in a snarl and her teeth are bared threateningly at Craig, but her tail is wagging furiously. She lets Craig get the stick and flings herself at him, her paws on his chest, and tries to lick his face. He laughs and nuzzles her ears. My dog. My boyfriend.

Click two – Craig going mad at Ari's party. The night Kobir died. Throwing himself about until there was no room for anyone to dance. Then hurling himself on Liam and shoving him up against the wall. His fist pulling back.

Click three – Romey, hanging in the swing high up out of my reach. Layla and me throwing ourselves at Meatface. Romey's terrified face.

Click four – Warwick's photograph of Craig on the railings at the vigil. Shouting and yelling with his mates.

Everything is turning purple. My body is one huge screaming lung. I shoot to the surface and suck in air in choking gulps. When my breathing has calmed down a bit I paddle into a patch of sunshine in the middle of the pool and float on my back in the warm water. I can feel sunlight on my skin and as I bob about I try to imagine I am floating in the bay in Trinidad where Kendra's great-grandad grew up. She's told me about it enough times. But the lap of the waves on the beach and the hot white sand under the coconut palms won't come. What I see in my head is still Warwick's picture of the vigil, and Craig and his mates yelling from the railings.

And I know what I have to do.

Warwick is in the street helping Denver unload crates of fruit from his van. I ran so fast to get to June's I can hardly speak. I grab his jacket to slow him down and gasp, 'Warwick. I've got to look at that photo again! The one of Craig.'

Warwick shakes me off. 'You off your head or what, Caryn? Can't you see Denver an' me are workin''.'

'Warwick, please. I wouldn't be asking if it wasn't really important.'

'Caryn, what you want me to do? Drop these bananas in the street? We'll be through in fifteen minutes.'

I can't argue. I sit outside on a milk crate, light a ciggie and have a Kit-Kat. When the last crate is unloaded, when it is stacked in the storeroom, when he and Denver have finished their chat, when he has shut the driver door, patted it and waved goodbye – then Warwick wanders over, taking his time at every step.

'I thought you were going to watch Denver till he disappeared into the sunset,' I grumble.

'Caryn, what is this? What do you need them photos for? . . . Dad, give us ten minutes, yeah? Caryn's here. I want to show her my pictures.'

June sticks his head out of the door. 'Hey, Caryn! How ya doin'? School finish early today?'

I show him the good side of my face. 'That's right, June. Training day for teachers.'

June grins and throws me a chocolate bar. 'A new line. From America. Tell me what you think.'

The pictures are still in their envelope. 'Just don't touch them!' says Warwick as he edges his bum on to the milk crate next to me. 'They got fingerprints on them already. Pick them up by the edges!'

Craig is in two of the pictures. Warwick and I look at them together. Eight guys are hanging from the railings above the crowd, on the wall that separates the hospital forecourt from the street. They are all wearing black jackets and some of them have caps pulled down over their eyes. One of them is

Craig. I know it is Craig. He is wearing a cap, but it is pushed to the back of his head. Craig is punching the air with one hand and yelling. They are all punching the air and yelling. They are really going for it too. Tense, rubbery mouths stick out from their faces like the open ends of condoms; the tendons in their necks are out like wires.

'What do you think they're shouting?' I ask Warwick.

Warwick gives me a funny look. 'I wouldn't know, Caryn. He's your boyfriend.'

'Can I take one of these pictures?' I ask. I want to show Craig the picture. I want him to look right at himself shouting and yelling and then try and say that it's not him. And I want to hear what he says next.

'Caryn, slow right down. What d'you need my picture for? Are you gonna do what I think you're gonna do?'

'I can't tell you now, Warwick. But I will tell you soon. And I will bring it back. I promise. Please?'

'Caryn. I wasn't born yesterday. I see what that picture says too. I should'ave seen it before, but I didn't sit down and take a good look at it like I done just now. You sure you're doin' the right thing now?'

I nod. What choice do I have? Looking after Tyler for his sister, that's what he said. Carrying the picture in its brown envelope, I go to find him.

19
CHEWS

'Babysitting? It's the first I've heard of it.' Craig's sister sounds suspicious when I tell her I'm ringing because I've forgotten the number of her flat.

'I never asked him to babysit,' she says. 'Not this afternoon. But come over anyway. You can sort it out when he gets here. He should be back soon. Twenty-five Lander Point. On the eleventh floor. Take the left-hand lift.'

Lander Point is miles away, down by the river in Limehouse. I have to take two buses, and it still takes me an hour to get there. It's a square white block that must be twenty storeys high.

She has the door open as I come out of the lift. 'I was watching from the window,' she says. 'I'm Sandra. I knew I'd recognize you. He's told me a lot about you. I can't wait to see his face when he finds you here. I hope he's not messing you about. I'll sort him out if he is. Tea?'

She's skinny like Craig, with the same funny eyes, only her hair is hennaed which makes her eyes look bluer. She's wearing jeans and a black top, with about ten chains round her neck. While we are waiting for the kettle to boil she gives me the once over and then she says, 'If he is messing you around, he's even dafter than I thought he was.'

The kitchen smells sour, of washing that hasn't dried properly. There is a basket of washing on the table in front of me and another one on the work top. Baby clothes and tea towels hang from the radiators, and a cot sheet is folded over the back of my chair. While I dip ginger biscuits in my tea, Sandra moves round, shaking little garments and tugging them into shape. First she asks me loads of questions about myself, and then she tells me about Craig.

'He's at his nan's', she says. 'He gets her shopping for her on his afternoon off. He's a good lad – I'm glad he's got himself a girlfriend. He needs to have some fun. Where did you two meet up?'

'At the rec,' I say. 'He told me what was wrong with my backstroke.'

Sandra laughs. 'Sounds like Craig. He's a sports fanatic. Here, have another gingernut.' She lowers her voice as if she's letting me into a big secret. 'He talks about you, you know. He's never talked about a girl before.'

I am beginning to loosen up. She has a warm, husky voice and a big smile, and part of me is looking forward to matey chats – even though I'm dreading what Craig will say when I show him the photograph, which is in my bag under the table.

'He shouldn't be too long,' says Sandra. 'He usually keeps his nan company for a bit. Ever since the mugging she won't go out by herself, so she doesn't see many people. He's very close to her. When he was a little kid he saw more of her than he did his mum. Went there every day after school. Stayed over two or three times a week. I was older, of course. Nan and I didn't get on. You know. Too much make-up, not enough skirt. And she hated my music. You should've heard the names she used to call me.'

'I never knew she was mugged,' I say. 'Was she hurt bad?'

'Knocked about a bit. You don't have to be hurt bad at her age. She's never got over it, poor old dear. Doesn't go out of the house any more.'

'Did they ever catch the people who did it?' I ask, not as if I really want to know. It's just one of those things you say.

She gives the sleepsuit she is holding a vicious tug. 'They were two black blokes – so the police didn't even try. You know what it's like round here. The blacks get away with murder. Dealing in the street. Guns. In broad daylight. The police know better than to arrest a black bloke.'

Blacks! She's not like that, is she? She's really nice! And we've been getting on all right! And then again . . . I think . . . well . . . maybe . . . if her nan was mugged . . . and I try to think of something that will let us start all over again.

'You've got a lovely flat,' I say.

It doesn't work – it just sets her off on another tack. 'I had to wait four years for this flat and I was born round here. Two streets away from where I stand to be exact! But that don't count for nothing these days. I was pregnant with my second before they give me this place. But other people – and we all know who – come over here and get given five bedroom houses straight away. Do you want another cup of tea?'

STOP! I want to shout. But I can't speak. I walk over to the window and look out so she can't see my face. Sandra thinks I agree with her! She thinks I go along with all that racist crap. Nobody comes out with that stuff unless they think you are on their side. And why does she think I agree with her? Because I go out with Craig of course!

I know where Craig is coming from now. I don't have to ask him what he was doing at the vigil. I know. Craig was at the vigil with his racist mates to make trouble. To start a fight. To ruin it for Kobir's family and friends and all the people who wanted to give him their hope.

My heart is thudding against my ribs. I feel sick. I ought to run. Get out before Craig gets back. Get away as fast as I can. But my legs stay rooted to the spot. Something still doesn't add up – it is nagging away in a corner of my mind and it won't let go.

The view from the flat is stunning. I can see the river winding in a great silver loop round the Isle of Dogs and the silver stripes of water that are the old docks. In the distance is the green of Greenwich Park and the domes of the observatory on the top of the hill.

'What a lovely view,' I say. Not that it matters what I say any more.

'What use is a view to me, with two kiddies?' she says. 'What do they take me for, a pigeon? But I'm not a Paki with nine kids, am I? I'm only . . .'

I'm saved from another rant by some sneezy, snuffly sounds that come from the pile of washing on the work top, then the whole heap begins to lift into the air.

'Oh, there goes Tyler!' Sandra leaps to her feet and shoves the washing to one side to lift a crumpled, red-faced baby from a carry cot. 'He won't go down in the afternoon like he used to. He only dropped off half an hour ago so I stuck him in there.' Tyler rubs his eye and starts to grizzle. 'He'll kick up if I don't feed him and I've got to get Jade from her friend's in two minutes.' Her eyes fix on me. 'You said you were coming to babysit. Can you give him his bottle while I get the girl?'

What could I say? Tyler and I don't take to each other. He is a blobby, red-faced baby of about nine months. He wails when Sandra goes out, but when I show him his bottle he shuts up, grabs it with both hands and starts to feed himself. I stick him in his chair in front of the telly – and go to see if I can find any answers.

Craig's bed is a mattress on the floor of Tyler's room, squeezed in so tight that one side curls up the wall. The black zip-up jacket he was wearing at the vigil is hanging from the picture rail, with a couple of shirts and a leather jacket I haven't seen before. A West Ham poster is blue-tacked to the door. A pair of leather boots and a new pair of Adidas trainers are lined up neatly between the bed and the door. The rest of Craig's stuff is in plastic bags on the floor underneath the cot. It doesn't take long to go through it. Trackie tops and bottoms in one bag. Jumpers in another. Two pairs of Levi's. Shirts. T-shirts. Underpants. Swimming trunks. A black belt with a heavy buckle. All clean and neatly folded. It doesn't tell me anything.

Books and papers are piled on top of a low wooden box under the cot that is Craig's makeshift bedside table. To reach them I have to lie down flat on the bed. I can feel the shape of his body in the mattress and I wriggle down into it. The pillow smells of his hair, and for a second or two I let go, and lie there breathing in his smell. Then I snap myself back and check out the books. Nothing there either. Two body-building magazines. I have to laugh. Craig has a long way to go before he looks anything like the guys on the covers. A book on electronics. A week-old *Evening Standard*, open at the football.

Tyler is shouting for attention in the next room and whacking his chair with his bottle. Sandra has made a nice room for him. A mobile hangs over the cot – brilliantly striped fish, swimming in the breeze from the open window. A shelf with teddies and a cuddly penguin. An alphabet frieze. And someone has stuck Union Jack stickers over the faces of some of the West Ham players. The black players.

It's time to go. Sandra will be back any minute now. I am putting all Craig's stuff back exactly like it was under the cot when I see another plastic bag, shoved right into the farthest corner, up against the wall. It didn't get there by itself. Someone hid it there. Deliberately. I worm my way under the cot and haul it out. It is bulky, but not heavy, and someone has twisted the plastic round and round before knotting it so that it is tightly stretched over whatever is inside. I almost break a nail on the knot before I bite into the plastic and rip it open.

Inside are a pair of Nikes – not new, but not old either. Something has been spilled all over them. Craig must have put them away until he has time to clean them. Whatever it was has dried to a dark, browny colour. *Blood*, says a voice inside my head. Shut up I say, of course it's not blood. *Blood*, says the voice.

Blood is crusted in the creases over the foot, in the weave of the laces, in the eyelet holes and in the design on the soles. It has soaked into the padding round the ankle and into the insole. Whoever lost it had been pumping out blood. His blood streaming over the ground. All over the cobbles of Canal Road.

I don't have to work it out. It all slides into place. Every question has an answer now – the same answer. Craig was one of the guys who battered Kobir – who killed him. Craig was in the white transit when it followed me. How did they know where I lived? Craig told them. How did they know where I worked? Craig told them. How did they know where I went to school? Craig told them. How did they know Layla and I were taking Romey to the park? Craig told them. Layla was right. I was under constant surveillance – Craig's.

I sit on the edge of his bed, totally paralysed, a blood-stained trainer in each hand. I have never felt this weird. This horrible. I feel peeled. Like a tangerine. My skin ripped away. My squishy inside shrinking from the air. Dreading whatever is coming next.

I am still sitting on his bed when I hear the sound of a key in the front door and Craig's voice calls, 'Sand. It's me.'

Tyler gives a yell, and Craig's voice from the living room says, 'Tyler! What are you doing on your own? Where's Mum?'

Still with a blood-stained trainer in each hand, I walk into the living room. Craig is undoing the strap on Tyler's chair. I say, 'My little brother sounded a lot worse than that after your mates had finished with him in the park.'

'Caryn!' Craig leaps to his feet.

I say, 'You were there, weren't you.'

I say, 'You kicked Kobir's head in. You killed him.

You and the rest of your mates. And you came on to me so you could make sure I kept my mouth shut. You told them everything they wanted to know about me. It must have cracked you up – you and your mates.'

Craig looks at me for a long moment. His face is not giving anything away. 'You going to grass me up then?' he says.

20
ZUR 4 GEM

In loopy scrawl across the wall of the lift. With a heart. Allright, Gem? You stick with Zur, Gem!

Zur
is not a
mur-der-er

My boyfriend is a murderer. He killed a boy. He killed Kobir. I know. I've seen the blood on his shoes.

He–killed–Ko–bir. My foot crashes into the flimsy metal sheeting, crash–crash–crash–crash. Once for every syllable, then crash–crash–crash–crash, again and again, until the whole lift rings with sound and I am the clapper inside a clanging bell.

'You going to grass me up then?'

When Craig said that I just lost it. I went ballistic! Whooshes of pain and rage shot out of me like rockets and exploded in bursts of red stars. Before I'd had time to think, I'd whacked him round the head with one of his bloody trainers. I took my arm back as far as it would go and hit him with all my strength. It cracked into his skull with a noise like a fairground rifle.

Then I heard my own voice from a long way off, high and broken like a scream. 'You killed Kobir and then you pretended to like me just to save your own poxy skin! And you didn't care what happened to me one little bit! And I fell for it, didn't I? I really went for it! Talk about sad! Talk about pathetic! I bet you haven't stopped laughing yet!'

Craig started to say, 'Caryn, I never meant . . .', but I wasn't going to give him a chance to speak. I was shaking all over with rage.

'Shuddup. Shuddup,' I yelled. 'I'm not listening to you. I'm never listening to your lies again. And for your information, yes, I am going to grass you up. Because you hurt me. And shamed me. And you hurt my baby brother. And you killed Kobir and then you came on to me – on the same day! And . . . And when I think about you and me together it makes me want to puke!'

Craig was hugging his arms across his chest. His face, where I had hit him, was turning scarlet. He was standing forward on the balls of his feet, every muscle tensed and ready to go, and his eyes glittered at me under his drawn-down brows. Did he think I was going to go for him again? Or was he going to go for me? He was supposed to be my boyfriend and I didn't have a clue what was going on in his head. I wasn't waiting to find out! My bag, with all my stuff in it, was still under the kitchen table. I left it there and raced out of the room and out of the flat.

What have I done? The lift has hit the ground and through the open doors I can see out on to the forecourt of Lander Point. A hundred years ago Sandra spotted me from her window as I made my way across that forecourt to her flat. I know that Craig is watching out for me from the same window right now, his mobile clamped to his head. The rage that kept me screaming and shouting in the flat drops off me like an unzipped skirt. As soon as I step outside Craig will tell Rosie and the rest of the gang which way I am headed.

I don't have a clue what I am going to do. I don't know it round here. It'll take me an hour to get home, maybe longer. I don't have money for fares. I don't have my mobile to phone Dad or Uncle Al. They are still under the table in Sandra's kitchen.

Somewhere, not far away, Rosie is getting into the transit. He is putting the key in the ignition. He is starting the engine. He is driving like the total mad-bastard, maniac nutter that he is to get here – on the wrong side of the road, through red lights, on pavements, up one-way streets, over round-abouts. He's probably taking a short cut through Mile End Park right now. No way is he going to stand back and let me walk into a police station.

My legs refuse to move out of the safety of the lift. I need a safe place to think. To work out a plan. Two guys with council jackets and toolbags are running towards me waving 'hold it' with their free arms. As they jump into the lift one says, 'Ta, love.' The other says, 'Seventeen please.' A place to think? Where no one is going to think to look for me? Why not? I press the button and we go up.

The emergency stairs window on seventeen is all smeary and I have to wipe it with my sleeve to see out. The main road, where I got off the bus, slices the area in two. Between me and the road is the railway viaduct. All the arches are blocked off, except one. I'll have to find it if I ever want to get out of here. To one side I can see water and boats, to the other, the massive traffic intersection at the Isle of Dogs. Over the main road, the streets loop round on themselves like a maze, squashed in by railways and canals.

It has gotta be the main road then. And that's where Rosie will be. Cruising up and down, waiting, watching, by the railway arch, by the side-turnings, till he plucks me off the pavement and throws me into the back of the white transit.

And if I make it out of here what will he do? Give up? No chance! He'll set off for my house and he'll wait on the corner of my street till I turn up.

But I have other places I can go. Dad's. Or Layla's. Craig never found out where they live. I can turn up there any time. I can ring the police when I'm ready – then I can just stay put.

Then, as soon as I turn my head towards Dad's, the answer hits me in the eye! A shining stripe of blue, straight as a pencil. The old navigation canal from the River Lee to Limehouse – where Dad walks Mango on summer evenings when I stay over. It'll take me under the roads and behind the buildings straight to Bow, and then I'm five minutes away from Dad's.

I've wasted too much time. I'm down the emergency stairs three at a time and out on to the forecourt. The sensitive spot in my back fizzes into life, telling me that Craig is following me with his eyes as I run down the steps and set off in the direction of the railway arch.

I cut off down the nearest street that has buildings high enough to hide me from his eyes. An alley takes me in the direction of the canal. Out the other end, my way is blocked by a terrace of old houses. The canal is behind them, but they are a rock-solid wall with no way through. I can hear the rumble of traffic on the main road, where Rosie will be waiting. I run away from the noise, but I am running back to Craig.

In front of me a woman is hosing down her car. Her front door is open and light is shining through the house from open garden doors. I don't stop to think. I am through the house, across the lawn and into the shrubs at the other end. Spiny bushes tear at my clothes and angry voices follow me as I crash down the other side of the garden wall on to a muddy bank and slither down on my bum on to the towpath.

Flat brown water. Ducks. Reeds. The end of the Limehouse Basin. I run away from the house along the canal. Round a long bend, the main-road rush-hour traffic squats on top of a low bridge. No white transit. I take a quick breather and look round.

Under the bridge, the canal narrows, elbows round sharply then continues dead straight under bridges – I can't see how many. The water sucks and slurps at the corner and the surface is whipped into waves by the wind. Debris scutters by on the current. Blank walls, the backs of factories, yards and works line the path for as far as I can see. Deserted wharves and loading bays rise straight out of the water on the other side. No one is about. Not a single fisherman, jogger, or dogwalker. Maybe this wasn't such a good idea after all.

I begin to run. Leaping bollards and skidding on the gravel, I run. Not too fast. Steady. I need to go the whole distance. I need to be outa here.

When two bridges are behind me I begin to feel safer. I begin to relax. I know where I am. A long stretch to the next bridge and one after that and I am in Bow, nearly at Dad's. I can almost smell Dad's crusty bread – with apricot jam, and yoghurt. I'm starving. Famished. I jog on slowly now. I can hear some lads playing footie in one of the yards on the other side of the canal. I'm not alone any more.

I'm close enough to see the brickwork on the next bridge when they stroll out. Two of them, Wobbler and Meatface, leaning on the parapet, waving at me. I stop dead, ready to sprint back the way I've come, but I already know what I'm going to see when I turn. There on the bridge behind me, the white transit.

I have played right into their hands! I am in a trap! I run back along the towpath to put some distance between us. They don't even bother to follow. When I turn to look, they are still leaning on the parapet, laughing.

There has to be a way out of this! An alleyway! A hole in the wall! I look down at the water. Forget it, Caryn! A sheer drop of six feet to filthy water. And no steps, no ladders the other side. I walk slowly along. The white transit gets closer with every step I take. Wobbler and Meatface are having the time of their lives.

Through the arches of the bridge they are standing on I can just make out the figure of a lone fisherman, too far away to be of any use. Then I remember the lads playing football and I race along the path until I am opposite their yard.

'Help!' I shout. Nothing happens. I shout again, still nothing. I yell, 'Rape!' so loud it rasps the back of my throat. A row of heads appears on the top of the wall.

'Where is he then, love?' one of them calls. His mates fall about laughing.

I point to Wobbler and Meatface on the bridge. 'They're after me. I'm scared what they'll do if they catch me!'

'What's this, rape by satellite?' shouts a wiseguy.

'You have to get closer than that, know what I mean!' shouts another. Then they roar, 'Right, mate!' at the bridge and go back to their game.

That's it! I plonk myself down on a bollard. If this is the way it's got to be, they can come and get me! I'm not going to walk into their arms! They haven't moved from the bridge yet – they're playing games with me. This is their idea of fun. I look down into the murky waters of the canal. What are they going to do to me? Throw me in? Hit me on the head and let me drown? They are killers, aren't they? But would they be that stupid? It would be the end of them.

I have to get myself over one of the walls. Somehow. There must be a way. I walk slowly back towards Wobbler and Meatface, hanging my head and trailing my feet, letting them enjoy the picture of me walking into their arms.

No wonder I missed it the first time. You'd have to be desperate. Between the adjacent walls of a yard and a factory, a minuscule gap. Bricks chipped and worn on the yard side, mortar rotten at the edges. But a chance!.

I jam the toe of my trainer into the gap. Knee high. Hard. It sticks. I push up and the other foot finds a worn brick higher up. I scrabble around with a hand for something to hold on to. Nothing. My hand shoves itself into the crack in front of my face, wraps itself round the brick corner and pulls sideways. The other does the same – and I am pulling myself up. My back foot comes up and kicks a shower of mortar out of the crack and I leap for the top of the wall.

I throw myself over it. Wobbler is pounding down the path towards me. His mate has disappeared. Over the wall is a yard, stacked high with palettes, backing on to a building. A locked, shuttered, barred building.

What happens next is all worked out for me. I don't waste time thinking about it. I jump down from the wall into some thistles that are growing out of a patch of cinders – then I'm off across the yard to a tower of palettes. I'm up them like a ladder and from the top I can jump for the next wall. I catch it with my hands and scrabble my way up.

The next yard is divided into two. The canal side is derelict. The other side is a car park to some low-rise flats. I trapeze my way along the wall and jump down into the car park. Get your belly over that lot, Wobbler!

An archway leads on to the street. It is all so normal I nearly cry. Kids on micro scooters. A guy working underneath a car. Traffic on the road.

I'm not sure where I am and I am trying to get my bearings when a massive weight hurtles into me from behind knocking me off my feet. I should fall, but I don't. I can't move a muscle. I am being crushed by pumped iron. I can't turn my head to look at his face, but I know it is Meatface. He sits down on the low wall that runs round the flats, pulling me down on to his knee. One iron arm is round my middle. The other is round my face, covering my mouth and pulling my head right back. I struggle. I wriggle and squirm. He wraps himself round me even tighter. I kick and he locks a leg over mine. I try and sink my teeth into the arm that is round my face, but I just end up with a mouthful of nylon. He squeezes me so tight I can hardly breathe and buries his face in my neck so we look like any other snogging couple.

We don't have long to wait.

21

PLUG TOUGH

The white transit thumps up on to the pavement in front of us. I don't see it coming – Meatface's arm is still round my neck and my chin is pointing at the sky. He jerks me to my feet, yanks open the back door and swings me inside like a bag of rubbish he is chucking into a skip. I land on all fours on hard metal. The door slams and Meatface climbs in. In the driver's seat, I get glimpse of a ponytail and an ear full of spikes, and we shoot off.

I am not alone in the back. Two young guys are lounging on piles of stuff, grinning at me – not in a good way. One of them is Jason Cook. When I try to sit up his mate boots me down. I sit up again. He boots me back down again. I give up and lie on the floor. We drive. Every time we go round a corner one of them boots me – but he pretends he lost his balance and his feet slipped. They both go, 'Sorry, sorry! I do apologize! I'm so clumsy!' in pretend posh voices and they think this is so funny that they collapse in giggles. So funny that they do it all over again. Half an hour of this and I am black and blue.

When the transit stops it is Wobbler who opens the doors and hauls me out. As soon as I am upright he grabs an arm and twists it up my back. It's my bad shoulder, and it hurts worse than a Chinese burn. I want to cry out but I choke it back – I'm not giving him the satisfaction. I don't even think of yelling for help. Wobbler won't think twice about breaking my arm – and anyway, there isn't any point. There is no one around to hear.

All around me are green fields. Ponies pull at the long grass. Chickens scrabble in the dirt. Goats, up on their hind legs, are munching away at the leaves of a conker tree and a black sheep is scratching itself on the fence. For a couple of seconds I think I must have lost track of time in the transit and we've driven all the way to the country, but then I look up and see the buildings that crowd round the edge of the field – flats, a church, and beyond them the city towers that I can see from my bedroom window. In front of me, raised up above the streets on brick arches, are the electrification cables of the main-line railway. I sort of know where I am – it's not somewhere I go, but it's not all that far from my house.

Wobbler shoves me along a cobbled, pot-holey road that leads to one of the arches, a black 'U' shape stamped on the brickwork. I can hear the others following behind. Wobbler has twisted my arm so far up my back my fingers are just about on my neck and if I stumble I'll wrench it out of its socket. My heart is a fist pounding at my ribs as if it wants to get out.

Is this it? Is this where they are going to do whatever it is they are going to do to me? How long have I got? Minutes? Seconds? I try to drag my feet but Wobbler gives my ankle a sharp kick. I roll my eyes round and round in their sockets to cram them full of everything there is to see. If these are my last seconds on earth I have to make them last.

Now we are under the arch. A stink of piss and dust – then Wobbler twists me right round to the left and I see, set into the wall in front of me, another arch. A person-sized brick arch around dense blackness. Velvety blackness I could reach out and stroke – that would wrap me into its folds and disappear me forever. Wobbler shoves me into it. My foot finds the first step and I climb up.

The darkness is full of rustlings and scratchings. Webby stuff sticks to my face and hair. My feet find horrible things. Soft, clothy things. I try not to think what might live in this place. On the bend of the stairs I stumble into something large and lumpy, which gives to my foot. Gives a little, but not too much. Light from above is greying the darkness now, but no way am I going to look down and see what it is.

Another shove from Wobbler and I am outside. He lets me go. He doesn't have to hold me any more. There is nowhere for me to go. We are standing on a crumbly track-way on top of the arches. Railway stuff, sidings or loading yards. On one side is a thirty foot drop to the field. On the other is a massive hole – the cutting where the trains creep along beneath the streets to Liverpool Street station.

This is it. They are going to toss me on to the tracks, into the path of a train. My heart is still hammering and now I start to shake. My knees give way and my hands grab uselessly at the air as I stagger forwards.

'Hnnuh! Nnhuh! She's shitting herself!' Jason Cook's mate. Laughing at me.

'Shut it!' The words were spat not spoken. 'Respect I said, didn't I? Whatever we think of the company she chooses to keep, the Paki-loving little tart is still one of us. Now where's that ladder? Or are we going to wait here all night?'

Rosie is standing at the top of the steps. Behind him, lights are going on in the city towers and the sky is streaked with red. His eyes are burning my face. 'Caryn MacSween. You and I have to have a chat. When the lads are done.' He jerks his chin at something behind me. 'Oy! You two! Move it!'

I had sort of seen the building as I came up the steps, but I hadn't really taken it in. A concrete box perched on high, narrow stilts, next to the tracks. A box with a pitched roof, windows and a front door that opens on to a small platform. I don't have a clue what it is. Jason and his mate are raising a ladder that had been lying on the ground, and leaning it against the platform. I know what is going to happen next. Jason runs up the ladder and opens the door. Wobbler shoves me forward. 'Move!' he says. It is the first time I have ever heard him speak.

On the ladder my knees flap like tea towels in the wind. I am already as high as a three-storey house and now I am climbing higher. The field is lost in dark-blueness way below me and the cutting is a gaping black gash. I climb higher and higher. I am so high I could be flying – and then the weirdest thing happens. It's like my head switches my body off. I no longer feel a thing. My heart calms down. My legs stop shaking. My head clears – and I stop climbing and look around me. Like Kate and Leo in *Titanic*, I lift my arms and stretch them out to the side. And I feel the space beneath my feet.

'Oy! What do you think you are? A friggin' eagle? Just get on up there!' Wobbler yells and the ladder judders as he lands on the bottom rung.

Inside the hut are bare concrete walls. A table. An old typewriter. A filing cabinet. Chairs. A settee covered in the England flag. A darts board. Empty cans round a bin. The stink of old fags.

Wobbler shoves me down on to a chair by the table. Rosie sits himself down opposite me. Meatface stands right behind him. Wobbler sprawls on the settee. Jason and his mate sit outside on the platform.

Rosie is leaning back, balancing his chair on two legs. 'So here's the interfering little bitch that's going to grass me up! The stupid little cow that thinks I am going to sit on my backside and let her tell lies to the police!'

A voice inside my head is saying, Don't act scared. That's what he wants. Be cool. So I look right back at him. His face is all straight lines. A downward slash for each eyebrow. Two slashes for the narrowed eyes and another one for a weird, folded-in mouth. He's old, the same age as my dad. Too old to be hanging out with Jason and his mate.

'Whatever you're planning, you won't get away with it,' I lie. 'Loads of people know why I was going to see Craig. Warwick in the shop knows. My mate, Layla, she knows.'

Jason has come inside and is sitting on the settee next to Wobbler. He doesn't meet my eye. I was at primary school with him. St Nicholas's.

'So, Miss Nobbynose, what are you going to tell them? That you saw someone getting a kickin'. A Paki gettin' what was coming to him. What he deserved. Now did you see me kick him? Did you see anyone in this room kick him? Could you swear? Did you see him?' He points at Wobbler. 'Him?' at Meatface. 'Him?' at Jason. 'What did you see then? You saw me watchin'? What's watchin'? Did you see me touch him? Nah! Did you see me lay a finger on him? Nah! Nah! Because I never did. I never laid a finger on him!'

The voice inside my head goes, Say you saw Wobbler. Say you saw Jason. But I didn't see them, not for sure. Wobbler maybe, the big guy who booted Kobir back down, but Jason, under the caps and balaclavas, I couldn't tell. Say you saw Wobbler – the voice in my head is firm and strong. My voice, when it comes out is high and whiny, like I am four years old. I point to Wobbler. 'I saw you,' I say. Then I point to Jason, 'And you.' And I look at Rosie. 'All right, you didn't lay a finger on him. But you beat him up with a baseball bat.'

Rosie smacks his chair down on to the floor and throws himself forward across the table so that his face is right up close to mine. His finger stabs at the air in front of my face as he hisses, 'And so what if I did? What if I did hit him? That wasn't a person you saw on the ground! That was a stinkin' piece of Paki shit! So what if he did get a kickin'? So what if he did die? He got what he deserved!'

His face is screwed up with rage and he has a twitch under his eye. He is mad! Crazy! Off the planet! And he could do anything!

Wobbler has got up from the settee and is prowling round the room. He walks and stops and walks and stops and when he gets to the door, he stands still, looking out. I can almost hear his brain ticking over.

Tell them about the pictures, says the voice inside my head. Tell Wobbler and Jason about the pictures.

'My friend Warwick's got pictures of you,' I say loudly, so Wobbler can hear. 'He took pictures at the vigil and he's got pictures of all of you.' I point at Wobbler, then Jason. 'He can show the police your pictures and tell them what you did to Kobir. Because I told him.' I point at each one again. 'You. And You.'

Rosie has calmed down and he sneers, 'That's right. Your friend's got pictures. Your black friend's got pictures! What's pictures? There was hundreds at that vigil. Pictures don't prove nothing. I never laid a finger on him. That don't prove nothing.'

'So if you never done nothing, why are you keeping me here then?' I squeak. 'What are you going to do to me?' The voice in my head is shouting, Don't say it! but it has tumbled out all the same.

It was a bad move. Rosie rocks his chair back on to two legs again. 'What are we going to do with you? We're going to teach you a lesson. You've been a bad girl, Caryn, and you've got to learn how to behave. You saw something you shouldn't've, right? Something you had no business seeing. And what do you do? Turn around? Walk away? Like any normal person woulda done? Oh no! YOU have to do it your way. YOU have to stick your nose in! What kind of person does that, ay? Ay? I'll tell you what kind of person . . .'

'Get rid of her, boss.' It's Wobbler.

Wobbler wouldn't think twice about getting rid of me! A brick on the back of the head and tip me in the river. Or just dump me on the tracks. He wouldn't care!

Rosie looks up at him. 'Just let me handle it, OK, Mark. Everything's under control.'

Wobbler mutters, 'I'm not going down for a grassing little tart like her.'

Rosie shouts, 'Listen, trust me, will yer. Now siddown!'

Wobbler doesn't move. 'She's trouble, boss. Let me get rid of her!'

Rosie is on his feet. He comes up to Wobbler's shoulder. 'Get outa here! You stupid or somethin'? This is not some no-hope Paki shit here. This bitch is white. Anything happens to her and we're in trouble. Big time. OK!'

For a second I think Wobbler is going to hit Rosie, but he stomps off and disappears down the ladder.

So they're not going to kill me. But I'm not out of here yet. It's not over by a long way. Stay calm, Caryn. Stay cool.

Rosie turns to me, 'And you. You were gonna grass me up! Shop me to the filth! What kind of tart are you?' His voice is shrill and the words are coming faster and faster. His eyes spark with madness. The straight lines in his face are going blurry. His face is melting. The muscle under his eye is going like the clappers. He is a total nutter. That's what Craig kept saying. Over and over he tried to tell me. Craig is scared of him. I'm scared of him. But I'm not as scared of him as I was. He might be mad, but he is not dumb. Not dumb enough to kill me.

'What are you going to do to me?' Keep him talking. Time. On my side. My best bet. My only one.

'Tell her, Jason.'

'We ain't gonna do nothin',' says Jason, with a nasty grin on his face. 'We're just going to leave you here. We're going to go away and lock the door behind us. With you inside!'

'And we're gonna throw away the key,' giggles his mate.

And then they left! One by one, they disappeared over the edge of the platform. Rosie first. Then Meatface. Jason's mate stopped on the ladder and waved, 'Ta ta, darlin'! Be good!'

Jason was last. 'Jase,' I said. 'You're not going to just leave me here, are you? It's only a joke, isn't it?'

Without looking at me, Jason takes a key from his pocket.

'Jason!' I grab his arm and hiss into his ear. 'If anything happens to me you'll be in trouble. Big time. I'm white, remember. The police won't let up till they find me. And by the time your case comes up, you'll be old enough to go down for years.'

Jason stands still for a moment, the key dangling from over his finger. Then he mutters, 'Shut it, MacSween! Just shut it, OK!' and steps out of the door. I hear the sound of bolts being shot, voices, the *DHUNK* of the ladder hitting the ground, then nothing. Nothing but the rumble of trains.

22
solo alert

Dhunkkk-kk-kk! The echo of the bolt hitting home flies round the room. I gawp at the closed door in a trance. I can't believe this is happening to me. It's not true! I'll just close my eyes for a minute . . . let time unspool . . . and when I open them again I'll be outa here . . . home . . . in my room . . . The blare of a klaxon on the tracks beneath me jolts me back to now. My eyes snap open and fix on the closed door and the massive wooden planks and braces. It is true. I am a prisoner. A prisoner in a concrete box.

I throw myself at the door. I shake it with all my strength. Hit it. Kick it. But it doesn't give an inch. It is as solid as the concrete walls.

The windows. They have to be a better bet. I rush over to the nearest one and press my face to the glass, but I can't see a thing outside – only needles of light from the towers over the field. The whole window looks like it is covered on the outside with some sort of mesh stuff. I wrench and twist the handle, but it doesn't even wobble, and when I take a closer look I can see that the whole window and frame are one solid mass of rust. I'll never shift it. Not in a million years.

By now my whole body is fizzing. Bubbling with energy like a bottle of coke that has just been shaken. I have to move.

I roam round the room. Bounce myself off the walls. Hit them with my fists. My arms. My head.

I can't be stuck in here! I can't! There has to be a way out! Don't panic, Caryn! Do something! There's gotta be something in here that will get you out.

Walls – bare concrete. A wooden table. An ancient typewriter. A filing cabinet. A metal settee with the St George flag draped over the back. Three chairs. A Calor gas ring. Gas canisters. Tins of coffee and powdered milk. A jar with sugar in it. A water carrier. Dirty cups. Knives? No chance. Spoons? Plastic. Not a single thing I can use to get myself outa here.

The top drawer of the filing cabinet sticks. I wrench it open. Inside is typing paper, ribbon, two cans of Heineken, a pair of socks and a roll of posters. The second is full of papers. Neatly stacked in bundles. I lift them out and spread them out on the table. Leaflets.

I rip them up! Shred them into tiny pieces! Throw them up into the air and let them fall like snow! When I have finished the floor around me is white and slithery with paper. Then I pick up the typewriter. I want to smash that too – but the weight of it in my hands sends a message to my brain. It is heavy and solid. I could use it. Smash through the mesh, or whatever it is, when I get the window open.

The typewriter gets my brain going. The filing cabinet! The files are gone, but what about the metal runners? Strong metal bars like blades, to work away at the rust. A metal frame chair to smash the windows. A gas cylinder? The same – if it doesn't blow up in my face! Not much else. But it's a start. I'll get out of here! It'll take time – but I'll do it!

It's too dark to do anything now. I'll do more harm than good crashing round in the dark. I'll do it as soon as it gets light. Someone will be around in the morning. Feeding the animals. Jogging across the fields. I'll work on it in the morning. Someone will see me in the morning. They have to.

Suddenly I feel very tired. I sink down on the floor and rest my head on my knees. I hurt. All over. Everywhere. As soon as I am still I can feel pains all over my body. My shoulder, where Wobbler barged me into the lamp post and locked my arm up my back, is agony. My face has started to throb again. My head aches. I've skinned my hands and bruised my knees. Jason and his mate took care of any bits that were left. It feels like my body has been painted all over in different colours of purple and blue.

And I'm starving! How long can you live without anything to eat? Three days? Five days? What if I can't get the windows open? Is that what they are going to do? Leave me here until I starve? I lean back against the wall. Terrible thoughts fight for space inside my head. Why didn't I tell someone what was going on? I wish I'd told someone. I wish I'd told Warwick. I wish I'd told my dad. He'd find me. My dad would turn over the whole of East London to find me. But they said 'respect' . . . didn't they? Surely that means . . .? Yes, but for how long? They're scared too. Scared of me. Scared of what I saw. Don't go there, Caryn. Just don't go there, right. It's not good for you. Switch off! Switch off!

I sit for a long time in the dark and let the whoosh of the trains fill my head. The main-line trains go diddly-der diddly-der. The underground trains go duhguhduh-whhsh, duhguhduh-whhsh. Soothing sounds. Soothing rhythms.

Knitting together, drifting apart. The floor under my fingers is covered in grit. Whatever they used to do in this shed on legs, it wasn't very clean. I roll my fingers over it and feel it crunch.

Then it is pitch dark and I am still sitting on the floor. It is quiet now – the trains have stopped for the night. I feel weird . . . weirder than I have ever felt in my life . . . light and loose right through me . . . like my muscles are no longer connected to my bones . . . my limbs are coming loose and separating from my body . . . and even the atoms that make me are spinning apart and zooming off in different directions . . . and soon everything that is me will have drifted away and I won't be here at all.

I lie down on the floor with the table as a kind of cover, curl myself up like Mango and go to sleep thinking of my dog's silky fur.

An explosion of noise and bright white light and I am awake! Bolts are drawn back, a kick crashes the door open, bootsteps bound across the floorboards. This is it! They're coming to get me. A flashlight pencils round the room – I shrink away from the probing light into the darkness under the table.

A voice shouts, 'Caryn! Where are you? We gotta get outa here!'

Craig? Craig! It's Craig!

I'm on to my feet, crashing the table over with the typewriter on it and shouting, 'Craig! What are you doing here?'

He grabs my wrist, 'Later, Caryn, OK. Just move it! We gotta go!'

'Craig, what are you . . .?'

'Caryn! It's Mad Mark – the fat one. He's on his way. Or he will be soon. Before it gets light. Now move.'

Wobbler! 'Get rid of her!' That's what Wobbler said. 'Get rid of her!'

We slide down the ladder and run for the steps. Then, winding round the narrow street at the edge of the field – headlights.

I freeze!

For a split second we watch the lights getting closer, then Craig whispers – as if Wobbler could hear us – 'Over here, Caryn, come on. Move!'

But I can't move. I'm frozen. My legs refuse to work. Craig grabs my hand and tugs and I stumble along after him. He drags me into the deepest darkness underneath the building and shoves me down in the long grass, behind a stack of girders.

'Craig . . . What's going on?' but he's off, bounding over the humpy ground – leaving me there! 'Craig . . .!' I hiss, but he's too far away to hear.

It's pitch dark, but I can just make out what he is doing. Dragging the ladder out from under the building. Raising the ladder to the platform. Shinning up it. Shutting the door. Sliding the bolts and locking them. Lowering the ladder and tucking it back into its place. Slithering down beside me in the dark.

'He must have seen you?' My voice is just breath.

'Nah. He'd only see what's in his headlights. Shut it, now, right.'

A bulky body is emerging from the top of the steps.

Wobbler looks even bigger in the dark. He shambles over to the building, hauls the ladder out from underneath it, raises it to the platform and climbs up.

Craig is creeping underneath the building. He waits in the darkest shadow until Wobbler has climbed the ladder, opened the door and stepped inside. As soon as Wobbler is inside, he gives the ladder a massive shove and it falls to the ground.

Wobbler's dark bulk appears on the platform. We hear his roars of rage as we throw ourselves down the steps and run!

And run! And run!

Craig won't let me stop. We race along for what seems like forever, until the tearing pain in my side forces me to stop. I collapse against a wall and breathe . . .

A micromist of rain hangs in the air. I lift my face and let it spritz my burning skin. Above us, a pub sign creaks in the wind. Craig puts his arms round me and pulls me close to him. I let myself be pulled. Just for one tiny fraction of a second I let myself sag against his sweatshirt. But it is too late. It was too late a long time ago.

I wrench myself away and pound my fists into his chest. 'Why did you come? Why did you come and get me? First you tell them I'm going to squeal and then you come and get me! Why, Craig? What's going on?'

I must be hurting him because he grabs my hands and holds them tight. When he starts to talk it's all broken up as if he spoke Chinese not English. '. . . I panicked, Caryn . . . when I saw you standing there with my trainers . . . I thought, That's it mate! It's over. She hates you now . . . and she's gonna go to the police and that's you finished for good! So I called Davo . . .'

Davo? Rosie? Davo!

'And Davo said not to worry, he'd sort you out . . . he'd think of something . . . give you a real scare . . . maybe lock you up for a bit . . . "Show that snouty little cow what it's like to be banged up" . . .'

Lock me up! Give me a real scare! You didn't have a problem with that, Craig? That was fine with you?

'And then I got to thinking . . . Davo. He's mental . . . a total headcase. You never know with him. He don't always think things through . . . he might have come for you in the morning . . . or the next day . . . or he might have just forgotten about you . . . put you out of his mind. He could do that . . . put you out of his mind.'

His face is white in the light of the pub sign and he stares at the sky as if there are words to be grabbed out of the air, 'And I kept thinking about you . . . stuck up there in the dark . . . not knowing what was going to happen to you . . . I kept seeing your face . . . thinking how panicked you'd be . . . and I was going to come and get you, I swear, Caryn, I was . . . then Jason rang.'

Thinking about me up there? Seeing my face in the dark? How long were you sitting on your backside thinking about me in the dark, Craig? How long?

'Jason was in a right state . . . he gave me the key . . . he said everything was going pear-shaped . . . Davo had lost it . . . didn't know what to do next . . . Mad Mark was out of control . . . he was going to kill you, Jason said, and we would all go down for a long time. And he could do it an' all . . . he can't count the fingers on the hand in front of his face, but once he gets an idea in his head, you can't shift him . . . he's the one that jumped on the guy's head.'

'. . . we would all go down for a long time.' You said it, mate! That's why you came, you bastard, isn't it? A missing white girl is one kind of trouble. A dead white girl is like – massive!

This is so doing my head in! I wrestle my hands away from his. I don't want to touch him any more. 'So that's why you came to get me,' I shout. 'To save your own skin! Not mine! *Yours!*'

'No, Caryn. That ain't true!' He's shouting now too. 'I came because I care about you. I know you don't believe me but it's true. I didn't have to come. I took a risk, you know. If Mark had caught me I'd have been dead meat too.'

Care! Care! Care how? Let me think about that one. Threatened! Assaulted! Humiliated! Chucked around like a bag of old laundry! Kicked to bits with size fourteen Docs! Scraped along the ground face first! That's care, is it, Craig? I'll show you care, mate! I'll show you care!

I hit him – as hard as I can. 'Care about me!' I yell. 'Look at me! Look at my face! You told them where to find me! You told them everything about me – where I lived – where I went to school – you even told them I would be going to the park with Romey! Rosie always knew where I was because you were keeping tabs on me.'

'No! No!' He is shouting again. 'Caryn! I care about you. I do. I never felt like this about a girl before. I was gutted when I saw your face. They told me they wouldn't touch you. But I wanted a life too. I didn't want to go down because of what a bunch of no-hope tossers did. I want to make some-thing of myself. And if I go down now I got no chance.'

Suddenly I feel very cold and I hug myself to keep warm. 'Maybe Kobir wanted to make something of his life too,' I say. 'Maybe he didn't want to die because of what a bunch of no-hope tossers did!'

Craig looks down at his feet. 'Yeah. Yeah, I know. But at the end of the day, Caryn, it wasn't like a real murder. You don't have to get so worked up. It was only a Paki. Think about it. It's not like it was one of us.'

Something weird is happening to me. Again. It's like I have stepped outside my own body and I am watching it from across the street. Seeing a shudder run right through it at Craig's words. Seeing it take a step away from him. Seeing my face close tight shut.

'Not like murder, as in, not like dead?' I know I'm wasting my breath, but it rushes out of me all the same. 'As in he was only a Paki so he didn't feel fear? As in he was only a Paki so he didn't feel pain? He was only a Paki so he didn't mind dying. Is that what you mean? He was sixteen, Craig. And you killed him.'

Tears are pouring down my face. It's Craig's turn to step back from me. He shoves his hands into his pockets and gives his shoulders a shrug. 'They don't belong here. They should go home. I mean, I never wanted the guy to die, but you have to show them we don't want them over here. Everyone thinks that. Anyone who don't is just kidding his-self. That's what I think anyway.' He chews at the side of a finger and looks up at the pub sign swinging in the wind. It is beginning to get light. '"We anchor in hope". That's a laugh!

You still going to the police?' I nod my head. 'I'll walk you home,' he says. 'King Kong might have swung himself down from the platform.'

I stare at him. 'I'm not going to leave anything out, you know. I'm going to tell them everything – the whole story – and that means you.'

Craig says, 'It's gotta come out, Caryn. I'm stuck with that lot for the rest of my life if it don't.' He turns and gives me a wobbly sort of smile, 'And I don't want that.'

We walk in silence through the deserted streets. It's drizzling like the first night we went out. Almost two weeks ago. There is nothing left to say – until we get to my door, when Craig takes hold of my arm and turns me towards him.

'Caryn,' he says. 'There's something you have to know. I never touched him. I was there, but I never touched him. I made like I was kickin' him, but I never. I couldn't. I couldn't kick him, not even once. There was blood everywhere, so my shoes are covered in it, but I never touched him. You gotta believe me. D'you believe me?'

Believe you? What does it matter whether you kicked him or not? You were there, weren't you? Slipping and sliding around in his blood with your mates. Paddling in his blood. You were there! I don't give a toss whether you landed a kick on him or not! Being there is enough!

'I believe you.' I shrug.

'No, but do you?' he insists. 'You gotta believe me!'

'Sure,' I go. 'I believe you!'

He lets go my arm and raises it in a kind of wave. 'See ya. Seey'around!'

'See ya,' I say. Then I go into the house.

23
NOW
NOW HERE
NO WHERE

The cafe bar is dazzling. Brilliant. Jill's new halogen spots are the business. Darts of light fly round the room, sparking on the glasses behind the bar and the gleaming knives and forks already lined up on the tables. Uncle Al is still running round with a polishing cloth and Jill is fussing with place cards and candles. Rich herby smells float through from the kitchen where Dad and his dishy new assistant, Tariq, have been slaving away since six o'clock this morning. I'm struggling with a massive bouquet of exotic flowers that I want to look cool and sophisticated. When I've finally got them right I stick them on the bar, under the sign that says 'Caryn's'. We open in one hour.

The flash blue dress with the sequinned top that Dad bought me is hanging in the back. It's blue to match the sign, and the spaghetti straps show off the yinyang dolphin on my right shoulder. I've still got a few minutes before I need to change. Chill time! I help myself to a voddy and blackcurrant and check my reflection. My new face looks back at me from the mirrors round the walls. A skinny face – all eyes and mouth and make-up. Hair short and tousled like an old toothbrush. I'm not saying I don't like it. It's sexy, but it looks tighter, harder, like my whole face has been sprayed with extra-hold gel.

Four months! It's four months since the Monday morning I walked into the police station. Four months since that awful night. I still can't get it out of my head. The minute I slow down it all comes rushing back. I lie awake at night going over and over it in my mind. The shed on legs. The terrible, empty feeling when the door slammed shut. And all the stuff about Craig. I'm sort of coming to terms with it, slowly, but I can't forget. Maybe, when it is finally all over, I will be able to let it go.

I didn't go to the police straight away. I needed to get my head straight before I started talking. When I did I thought I'd be in and out of the police station in an hour or two. Dream on, Caryn! I was in there for ten hours. Five hours to talk my statement through. Five hours to write it up. And that wasn't the end. Nowhere near. There were the identity parades. And they want me to stand up in court. If I don't testify they won't be able to convict, and Rosie and his gang will walk free. So I said I would testify. After all, I've come this far. It doesn't make sense to back off now.

The court case is in a few weeks. Rosie and Wobbler are up for murder and kidnap. Meatface is up for kidnap. They are all up for interfering with witnesses. And Craig? Craig walked free!

Mum went mental when I turned up at a quarter past five on that Thursday morning. She'd been going out of her mind with worry. She was all geared up for a mega-lecture but when she got a good look at me she was like – Casualty! Doctor! Check-up! Now! All I wanted was something to eat, a bath and my bed. She heated up some soup, dolloped in Greek yoghurt and made me a cheese and tomato sandwich. I told her what had happened between mouthfuls.

When I got to the bit about Wobbler, she squeaked, 'Oh, Caryn, you don't mean . . .? He wasn't going to . . .?' and threw her arms round me and started to cry.

She got the details out of me while I worked my way through a carton of Cookies and Cream, chewing away at her knuckles until I could see toothmarks in her skin. When I had finished she sank her face into her hands and sighed, 'Caryn, I just can't believe that all this has been going on and I didn't know anything about it. Why ever didn't you tell me? What on earth did you think I'd do?'

'What did you want me to do? Write you a note?' It just came out, I don't know where from. The moment I saw her face, I wanted to unsay it – except for a tiny mean little bit of me that was smiling to itself – and in the end I kept quiet.

After that I crashed. I curled up in my bed, pulled my duvet over my head and let sleep flood into my bones. I woke up in the evening as stiff as a board and totally famished. Dad was there, cooking, and I could feel serious discussions in the air. I stretched myself out carefully on the settee. Mango jumped up next to me and shoved her nose into my sore ribs.

Dad was doing his nut. 'Who was he?' he demanded. 'Just tell me his name. I'll have him! I'll murder him!'

'Who?' I said.

'The one who did this to you, of course. Who got you in this state.'

Of course I had to go through it all over again. I never

said anything about Romey – I didn't want Dad to have a heart attack – and I didn't say anything about Craig. I made out that it was all down to Rosie and Wobbler. The mood Dad was in, he'd've probably gone round and sorted Craig out right then and, anyway, I didn't want to tell him. He'd find out soon enough. It was just too shaming to say it was my boyfriend all the time and I never had a clue. Even thinking about Craig now makes me curl up inside. I still can't believe I was that dumb! That it took me so long to connect.

It shut Dad up. Totally. He was gobsmacked. He shoved Mango off the settee and sat down beside me. He had his wooden spoon in his hand and he slapped it against the palm of the other hand as he spoke. It still had tomato sauce on it and he never noticed as it splattered on to his jeans. 'Why?' he said. 'Just tell me why?'

I'm like, 'Why what?' Thick as a brick.

'Why d'you do it, Caryn? What possessed you? Did you lose every single marble at one go?' There was a wobble in his voice. 'I could be looking at you on a mortuary slab right now! You know that, don't you? Your mum and I . . . You know what I mean. Why didn't you just stay out of it? Why risk your own neck like that? For a Paki?'

That really got Mum going. 'Don't start, Pete! Not now! I'm very proud of my daughter. She stood up for what she knew was right. I'm proud of her, but . . .!' Her eyes filled with tears again.

Dad got up and stretched an elastic arm round her shoulders. 'Yeah, you're proud of her, but you'd sooner she hadn't've done it. And I'm proud of her but I'd . . .'

'No! I am genuinely . . .' Mum was saying, but by

this time I had the oven door open. Homemade pizza, with chorizo and chilli. And plum and crumble. Bless!

'Dinner's ready!' I yelled. 'I'm starving!' That shut them up.

One thing they did agree on though – I was grounded. Under house arrest 24/7. Mum took a week off work and after that I went to stay with Dad and Jill. I ended up slaving for Dad in the cafe bar.

Layla came round on Saturday with a load of videos and CDs. She inspected my bruises, and then she got the whole story out of me. She'd wrapped my duvet round her shoulders and, as I talked, she gripped it tighter and tighter round herself until it looked like she was sitting in a little tepee. Her hair was all pushed up on top of her head and it tumbled forward over her eyes. I could just see the shine of her eyeballs through her hair.

She was on Dad's side. I knew she would be. When I had told her everything she stared out of her tepee at me for ages before she breathed, 'Shi-it! Caryn!' Then she stared again, and then she leaped to her feet, chucking the duvet on to the floor, and she hit me! She whacked me on my bad shoulder. Hard.

'Layla!' I yelled. I was gobsmacked. 'You hurt me! What you do that for?'

This time, she took hold of my shoulders and shook me. 'You're mad, you are! You could have been scarred for life. And I could have lost my best mate. You know that? You could have died. I don't want you to die.' This time she flung her arms round me and hugged me.

'Come on, Lay!' I said when I had untangled myself. I

was getting fed up with people telling me I was mad. 'You would have done the same if it was you.'

'No, Caryn, I would not! I'd have run the minute I saw that white transit. Like any normal person would. But you? You only stand there, right up where they can see you, and watch. And as for going round to Craig's house! What were you trying to do? Commit suicide?'

I didn't say it out loud. It sounded too pathetic. I went round to Craig's house because . . . because I wanted to be wrong about him. I was desperate to find out that he wasn't the person I already knew he was. I wanted to give him one last chance to be Craig, my boyfriend, who worked up the road. Who liked playing frisbee with my dog. Who'd cross the street if he saw Rosie coming towards him.

And up on Canal Bridge? Why did I turn round? That's the big one! It took me ages to figure that one out. As soon as I saw what was going on I hurried on, to get out of the way, to keep out of trouble. But there was another part of me that I didn't know existed then that woke up and said, Hey! You know what's going on down there! Don't let them get away with it! And for one second, that part was stronger and I turned and looked. Then, when Kobir died, it grew. And every time Rosie leaned on me it pushed back. *NO!* Until I knew that sooner or later I was going to shout it out. *NO!* Craig or no Craig – I would have said something in the end.

Rosie and Wobbler going down didn't change much. I keep getting phone calls. Grassing cow! We'll have you! We know where you go! And they're worse now the court case is getting close. Some joker has graffitied the rail bridge above the market, **Caryn MacSween is a grass!** What can you do? We take the phone off the hook at night, and I never let Mango out in the Fields by herself now. I never let her out of my sight.

It's not been all bad. Warwick's been there for me, and Ezra. Layla and Ari – big time! I've had write-ups in the local papers and sometimes flowers arrive on the doorstep. And Natalie! Natalie was round as soon as word got out. She walked out of the door in the middle of her mum telling her to stay right away from me. We're good mates now.

One thing. I never heard from Kendra. Not a word. When I phone her she hangs up, and she never replies to my texts.

I went back to school after six weeks. Natalie said don't go, and Layla said don't bother. I knew it was going to be bad – but there were things I needed to check out for myself. Like, for example, Kendra.

They knew I was coming. As I stepped through the gate the whole yard went totally silent. It was like switching off a radio. Every single kid turned to look at me. Pushed and shoved to get a better view. Between me and the main entrance was a solid wall of bodies, all staring straight at me.

Stare right back, said the voice inside my head. Don't act scared. Walk towards them. So I did, and a path opened in front of me – and then the hissing started, ssss . . . sssss . . . sssssssss . . . grasssssss . . . grassssss . . . grasssssssss. Then other words. Larraine nipped me on the back of the arm and I felt her boot on my ankle. Fingers poked my back, tugged at my hair. Boots kicked at my legs. Gary Cook shoved me, hard, into Aidan Coughlin, who shoved me back again. 'Go home, Grass!'

I never thought they were going to really hurt me. They didn't dare. Just hiss and poke and duck back into the crowd. But I could see the hate in their faces. Feel it in my churning guts. I definitely wasn't going to give them the satisfaction of turning back now – but the yard was getting bigger by the minute and I couldn't see how I was ever going to make it into the building.

Then the path through the crowd closed in front of me. And behind me. I was trapped. Panic fluttered through my guts. Then I saw Kendra's yellow head bobbing towards me. Kendra! My mate! Relief wiped everything but that one idea from my brain. My tonsils bulged with the effort of holding back tears – so much I almost choked. I shoved my way towards her. When I reached her Kendra's face was a mask.

'Grassing bitch!' she said. 'Grassing your own boy-friend!' And she spat. The gob of spit landed on my jacket.

Kendra spun round and stalked off through the crowd. She held herself very tall, and her long black coat swirled behind her as she walked. That was the last time I ever spoke to her. I always felt good when I was with Kendra. When I was with her I could feel the strength in myself. As she walked away, I felt my strength running out of the soles of my feet.

After that they let me go. The fun was over. They'd seen my face. That was enough for them – for now.

Inside the building, the first person I saw was Doherty, scurrying towards the yard to blow the whistle for beginning of school. She stopped dead in her tracks when she saw me. 'Caryn! What are you doing here?'

'I'm back,' I said.

'Are you sure you're quite ready to come back?' She was sounding concerned, but she didn't fool me. 'We weren't expecting you just yet.' She was stunned, I could tell. She's a cool old bitch most of the time, but she didn't know what to do with this.

'I'm fine,' I lied.

'Caryn.' She was walking back up the corridor with me now. 'I'm sure everyone would understand if you took some more time off. After all, we don't want to be asking for trouble, do we?'

That was when I understood. They hated me. All of them. Kids. Teachers. Black. White. They all had their reasons and they all hated me. They wanted me to disappear. I had rocked the boat. I had stood up against the crowd. I was making their lives difficult. I was making them ask questions. I was making them think.

I walked out of school then and I never went back. No one pressured me. Even Mum was off my case by then. All she said was, 'It's your life. Take your time.'

In my head I kept seeing Warwick's photographs. The ones he took at the vigil that told me all about Craig. And about Rosie's gang. I got to thinking that I'd like to take pictures that told people things they needed to know. So I talked to Warwick and I've signed up for a photo-journalism course at Layla's college.

Then Dad came up with his big idea. I was in the cafe bar putting a burnt-orange wash on the walls when he leaned on my ladder and said, 'Caryn's. I thought Caryn's, in neon. There's a guy in Bethnal Green who'll do us a sign. Anything we like. What colour would suit you?'

I didn't even stop painting. 'Like you want a brick through the window? The trial is in a few weeks, or have you forgotten?'

'How could I forget? I think about it day and night. And I'll never understand why you did what you did. In my book, you look after your own. But you did it. And you're my own. And I'm telling anyone that wants to know that I'm right behind you. Anything they do to my girl, they do to Pete MacSween as well. And if they've got anything to say to you, they're saying it to me too. You OK with that?'

I fell forward and caught his shoulders and he pulled me off the ladder and swung me round and round before dumping me down on to the floor. 'Blue! Blue! Blue!' I shouted. 'I love it! And I want it blue! But it's mad! Insane! You know that, don't you?'

'Too right I know!' he said. 'But I can handle it!'

Everyone has arrived now. Babaa Maal is on the stereo. The candles are lit. And here we are, among all the rest. Me. Mum. Dad. Jill. Layla and Ari. Bridget and Spiro. Natalie and Reuben. Warwick and June. Uncle Al and his mates. At the grand opening of Caryn's Cafe-Bar, under a cool blue sign. Waiting for the trouble to start. And when it comes, we'll handle it.